MIND THE DOORS

ALSO BY ZINOVY ZINIK

ZINOVY ZINIK

MIND THE DOORS

LONG SHORT STORIES

Context Books New York

Published in the United States of America
Context Books, New York.
Distributed by Publishers Group West

www.contextbooks.com

Designer: Johanna Roebas
Jacket design: Susan Carroll
Typeface: Garamond MT

Context Books
368 Broadway
Suite 314
New York, NY 10013

Library of Congress Cataloging-in-Publication Data
Zinik, Zinovii.
    [Short stories. English. Selections]
    Mind the doors : long short stories / Zinovy Zinik
        p. cm.
    ISBN 1-893956-04-0
    1. Zinik, Zinovii–Translations into English.   I. Title.
PG3490 . I495 A2 2001
891.73 ' 44–dc21
                                                        2001000767
"No Cause for Alarm" was translated and adapted from the
Russian by Bernard Meares and the author; an earlier version
of "The Notification" was published by Harbord Publishing
(London) in *One-Way Ticket;* both "The Notification" and
"Double Act in Soho" were translated by Andrew Bromfield
and adapted by the author.

9 8 7 6 5 4 3 2 1

Manufactured in the United States of America

ACKNOWLEDGMENTS

I would like to express gratitude to my publisher, Beau Friedlander, for the many suggestions and generous help in editing and improving the extant translations; to Michael Wojas, proprietor of the Colony Room in London's Soho district for providing essential background information, and most importantly to my wife, Nina Petrova, for understanding and tolerating my many absences and distractions.

CONTENTS

MIND THE DOORS

A PICKLED NOSE

Before Francis Bacon's portrait of Muriel Belcher was put up for sale, the auctioneers from Christie's arranged a private viewing for the press and regular patrons at the Colony Room. It was a clever idea, really, to bring the picture back to its birthplace. The late Muriel Belcher had owned Bacon's favorite watering hole (little water, much whiskey). The viewing was a cunning publicity stunt. Newspapers are constantly on the lookout for gossip, and Christie's people rightly recognized that a painting from Bacon's Belcher period, shown in the Colony, couldn't fail to attract attention.

Muriel Belcher had arrived in London after the war, having run away from both her native Birmingham and authoritarian father, who was a prosperous Jewish impresario of Portuguese extraction. Muriel was accompanied by her lesbian lover, a Jamaican named Carmel, whose colonial origins may have influenced the naming of the club when it opened in 1948. Britain's then retrograde licensing laws forced pubs to shut their doors in the afternoon, so heavy-drinking Sohoites would be forced to move next door with their glasses to private establishments such as the Colony. In those days Francis Bacon was neither rich nor famous. He made up for this shortcoming with a wide variety of rich and famous friends whom he introduced to the Colony, which got him free drinks in perpetuity. Bacon called Muriel "mother," and Muriel reciprocated by referring to Bacon as her daughter. A close and cozy family, indeed. Soon, they were joined by the entire London school of painters—or, rather, the drinkers of that school. A love of booze was the only artistic thing they had in common.

Soho is the very embodiment of all that is seedy and sensual, clandestine, illegal and brutally exhibitionist. It has long been the cognate of my tormented émigré soul. This square-mile magic island has for generations attracted to its shores all kinds of shipwrecked refugees and undesirables— French Huguenots and Spanish Jews, Italian anarchists and Marxist philosophers have all happily coexisted alongside the peddlers of sleaze and neighborhood nuns. Among this motley collection of outlandish types and sexual minorities, my displaced Muscovite-Londoner persona has always been perfectly at home.

Within the magic island of Soho, the Colony Room is a

separate state municipality, with its own borders, laws, and rituals, totems and taboos. Pretty much every drunk among the Soho diehards has a story to tell about the Colony, although many have never been inside. First, one has to find the entrance. This mysterious limen is squeezed between two nondescript restaurants (whose names and owners are constantly changing). The green door that leads to the Colony is usually camouflaged behind restaurant tables. This door opens onto a badly lit staircase, painted racing green. Climb two breakneck flights of stairs that pose mortal danger to life and limb, and one comes to another green door. Open it, and enter something very much like a theater set. Time has stood still for generations.

The walls and ceiling are quite predictably green. To the eyes of an Irishman, green is both the color of shamrock and race tracks. For the English, it is probably most like a snooker table. I don't know what the symbolism of this green signifies for the Chinese, but in the minds of Russian alcoholics like myself, it is the spitting image of the Green Dragon of vodka delirium. But whoever you are, the moment you enter the room, you are lost to the outside world as if hijacked to the green woods of some enchanted forest.

Every capital city in every civilization has a bar like this: a hidden entrance for the chosen few, a barroom crammed with dusty memorabilia, its row of tattered rickety stools taking up a third of the inevitably cramped room. The walls are plastered with photographs, paintings by "our great geniuses," old posters and pinups, framed newspaper cuttings referring to famous disturbances of the peace and public quarrels, old fan letters and postcards on the mantelpiece, pictures of "the inner circle" celebrating acts of outrageous behavior, crimes and misdemeanors, framed and unframed fragments of a glorious past—all of them like omens of a no-less exciting and scandalous future.

The window box looks like the frame for a work of pop art: From its arch hangs Muriel's patent leather bag and her lacquered walking stick. Her pale, ravenlike features and piercing gaze look down on the drinkers from numerous photos. Long since dead, she still manages to dominate the room. In her day, she was notorious for cutting short any cant utterance or snobbish gesture, and drowning the sacrificial tippler in a torrent of obscenities of such force that he or she often didn't dare turn up again. Ever since the days of her fierce reign, the Colony Room has upheld its shock-tactic tradition with newcomers, as if testing their moral rectitude and spiritual resistance by subjecting them to all manner of verbal abuse. It is the Soho version of Darwinism. Anarchists may be egalitarian, but even they have their own passport systems, hierarchical orders, and seats of privilege, not to be sullied by riffraff. Having said this, the Colony Room crowd would never have anything to do with Democracy.

Those accepted by the Colony Room never again feel lonely on this island. While the rest of England has tired of any general notion of human bondage, this enclave of incorrigible drunks, it seemed to me, managed to maintain a sense of belonging—to a tribal community, a secret society, or clandestine order of the chosen few. As a result, their sense of history has always been of a home-brew, samizdat variety, quickened with a taste of moonshine. Denizens of Soho—that separate nation—often express their sense of history through apocryphal accounts of drunken antics that eventually acquire the symbolic significance of state business. This was more so in the case at the Colony Club.

Part and parcel of those chronicles was, of course, the Francis Bacon myth. This myth could only have been created amid the feverish atmosphere of Soho during the postwar years. During that period, some of Soho's habitués, nourished on a diet of undercooked Marx and raw Freud marinated in champagne, were discovering the Nietzschean abysses of the human spirit in a whiskey glass. Others, like the atheist and iconoclast Bacon, were trying to rescue man from his own depths—tearing apart the body, grabbing his genitals to pull himself out from the abyss of his spirit.

Human anatomy has always played a major part in the Soho oral tradition. Every member of the Colony knows by heart the story of Bacon's fall down the stairs in the last throes of inebriation. Some stories say his eyeball popped out, but he shoved it back with a thumb. Others insist that it was not his eye but his nose that was put out of joint, but that he pushed it back into place with a single blow of his fist. He himself was so drunk that he couldn't remember whether it was his eye, nose, or right nut. Still, the details of the story matched the style and spirit of his paintings, disfigured bodies the color of raw ham in a nod to the origins of his name. (The rentboys of Soho called him "Eggs.")

Incidentally, Bacon's favorite book was an illustrated manual entitled *Diseases of the Mouth*. To my mind, these shocking anatomical obsessions concealed a passion to prove that we are nothing but self-made machines, and his sole desire was to break us open—to see the mechanism and how it works. Like all idealistic materialists, Bacon was anxious to lay bare the human soul to show, as if in an anatomy lesson, how spiritual muscles make emotional tissues move.

Bacon couldn't stand the sight of his own features. Those puffed-up cheeks made him look like a fat toad. The haunted expression of his eyes transformed the toad into a charming monster. He was one of those artists who spend their lives trying to discern their own image in alien things. Maybe homosexual cravings include the desire to see oneself in the mirror of another's eyes.

When we came face-to-face for the first time (ahead of his Moscow exhibition), our hectic conversation, lubricated by a bottle of Famous Grouse, left me feeling that he wasn't talking to me but through me—to himself—as if he was reacting not to my words but to the echo of his own thoughts. I might just as well have stood up and walked away, leaving him with a tape recorder.

I confused his defensiveness with the indifference of a dictator.

Every artist is a despot of a kind, like all tyrants. Bacon was particularly sensitive regarding his image in the eyes of others. He seemed almost to have a mortal fear of being taken for someone he didn't want to be, and of being unmasked as someone he didn't suspect he was. Paradoxically, that Godlike terror of a clearly defined identity made a ferocious atheist of him. The person who believes in his own uniqueness cannot believe in the existence of an afterlife. The existence of an afterlife implies that your life will be reshaped all over again in a similar vein. That, in turn, means that your life in this world, as a work of art, was a flop. After all, how can a work of art be regarded as unique and perfect if it can be repeated somewhere else, re-created and emulated by someone else, even if by the hand of God?

Bacon coaxed my own fear of being watched by cold and curious eyes. Yet as soon as the formal interview was over and the tape recorder switched off, his mood changed. I began speaking about my own idiosyncratic experiences as a Russian living in London, and witnessed the eighty-year-old tyrant with his childish tantrums transform into an inquisitive and clever child. He listened intently, laughed at every joke, and we quickly put away two-thirds of the Famous Grouse. The rest was polished off en route to the Colony Room, where we were to meet James Birch, who had organized Bacon's retrospective in Moscow. Birch was also known as "the Prince of Darkness" in Soho's nightlife. Birch was sensational in both roles. He was also the one who put me up for membership in the Colony.

"It almost looks like Bacon could see the future of Ian's nose in Muriel's face," I declared boldly. Ten years had passed since my first (and last) conversation with Bacon. The portrait of Muriel was on an easel standing next to the bar. It was positioned so the picture's background matched the wall, where there hung an enlarged photo of the real Muriel staring defiantly down at her painted image. The original clearly disliked the bulbous growth on the copy's face, which looked like an old shoe. It was, in fact, a dead ringer for Ian Board's nose.

Ian was Muriel's darling former barman. He had inherited the Colony Room, along with the unofficial title of Master of Ceremonies, or, better still, Master of the Unceremonious. Muriel had always used the Colony's chatterers as a multifaceted prompter, which gave her free rein to blurt out the most inventive obscenities. Some would say it was her own sophisticated way of entertaining her guests, rather than an outright humiliation. Ian, on the other hand, needed no prompting. He insulted the customers indiscriminately.

During my first few years in London, I used to visit the Colony for a kind of shock therapy: After withstanding the terrors of Ian's unpredictable verbal abuse at the club, I could embrace my estranged and depressing London existence like a homecoming. It took me years to realize that Ian Board had ingested all the bile and bitterness circulating among Soho's old-timers and metabolized it into the foul-mouthed persona of tetchy punkdom.

He used to sit on "Muriel's throne," a high stool situated not behind the bar but in front of it. It was tatty and worn-out, like the rest of the furniture at the club. Against the backdrop of the green-as-envy walls, Ian was the only spot of color. He used to dress like a flamboyant American beach bum, with his baseball cap, unthinkable jumpsuit pants, and a T-shirt. The tawdry colors matched the parrot in the toy cage by the window. But whereas the stuffed bird was quite dead, Ian was both alive and kicking—his customers, that is—and parroting their bawdy exchanges with horrible shrieks.

Perhaps the most striking resemblance between Ian and the parrot was something that anatomy books call a beak and a nose, respectively. The bizarre colors of Ian's proboscis made his jumpsuits look drab. That boiled mush of a nose was the stuff of legend, purple and porous, like a rotting eggplant. Shift your eyes to avoid the horrible sight, and you might pick out one of the numerous photos of Ian on the walls. The progress from decadent youth to semi-invalid debauchery reveal the passing years measured out by his mutating nose. He must have possessed a strong masochistic streak to put up with its daily decay. The mirrors duplicated the catastrophic changes. I wonder if Ian's merciless stance toward himself caused his legendary impatience with others.

"Hello, Miss Russia," he would blurt from beneath the peak of his cap, nostrils trembling (Ian's nose was a sensor for detecting newcomers). At such moments its scarlet colors reminded me of the Soviet flag. In fact, Ian had started to acknowledge my presence in the Colony only after a sharp exchange I had with Bacon on the subject of Eisenstein's Stalinist politics and his cinematic genius. Only then did Ian seem to realize that I was the only Soviet-born member of the Colony Room. Not as red as his nose, though. The nickname he invented for me—Miss Russia— contained the inevitable sexual innuendo. I wasn't the only one to suffer in this way. Even the *Spectator*'s cartoonist, Michael Heath, was dubbed Hampstead Heath, as if he had something to do with that infamous hot spot of gay activity in London. No one came near Ian without being exposed as a queer, an easy lay, a bum, a coward, or a pervert. Part of the family, that is. It was my dream, wasn't it? To become one of the family. A dream fulfilled. So every time he called me Miss Russia, I swallowed the insult with a faint smile.

Almost a year had passed since my last visit to the Colony, when we celebrated the anniversary of Ian's death. Drunken tears, shouts, hysterical laughter, songs sung out of tune. Now, the place was quieter. Otherwise, it was not much different. The crowd that came for the private viewing of Bacon's portrait gradually dispersed. Only the regulars were hanging on. Not unexpectedly, I was greeted by two familiar backs. One belonged to the bearded Malcolm, a producer of avant-garde and radical porn videos, and the other to the bulky Bill Greenberg, editor of the avant-garde and radical monthly journal *Engagement*. With his backside draped over the barstool, Greenberg looked like an exhibit from one of Malcolm's experimental porn shows, which, in turn, might have become the subject for an analytical review in Greenberg's radical magazine. Ostensibly dedicated to East–West dialogue during the Cold War, *Engagement* was subsidized by a number of the world Intelligence services (or so it was rumored), while its editor was engaged with Malcolm in the study of the human race, Eastern and Western, at nearby bars and parlors. The helix of their activities was a reflection of the local topography. Greenberg's offices were right next door to Malcolm's studio on Windmill Street. From time to time, respectable, bookish contributors to Greenberg's *Engagement* would absentmindedly get the wrong entrance. Afterward they would wonder why lining up to support freedom of expression had to make them party to the staging of alternative sex fests at their publisher's editorial offices. Greenberg was too busy to answer this burning question, because he spent most of his working hours with the Colony mob, smoking his anti-American Cuban cigars (evidently mandated by the name of our club).

This time they were all present: Tom and Steve, Susan and Sarah, and the charmingly petulant Big Eddie, constantly apologizing for the scandals she created but didn't remember. Hardly anyone could remember when, why, and with whom she had quarreled. The same Big Eddie once confessed to me that during her thirty years in the Colony Room, she could only recollect three hours when she was "accidentally sober." She was in no way sober now, and neither were the people from Christie's, who had stopped fussing over the painting and sat in amazement at the flow of obscenities that came as thick and pungent as the smoke from Greenberg's cigar. As usual, such epatage was aimed at shocking the outsiders, checking them out before letting them buy a round. At the Colony, you had first to be cruel to strangers before allowing them to be kind to you.

"Hello, Miss Russia," I expected to hear as usual, forgetting, in the familiar atmosphere of the Colony, that Ian Board was no longer among us. But his ghost was there. In fact, Board's back was there, too: the same old tawdry T-shirt, the same baseball cap. But the head was different. It swung round to reveal not Ian's rotten beetroot of a conk, but the sharp-pointed Gogolesque beak of Michael Wojas. Michael had installed himself upon Ian's throne. Michael's detractors had always been quick to label him a usurper whenever he sat on the stool during Ian's absences. And now that Ian would be gone until the Second Coming, the same malicious gossip peddlers drew attention to the fact that Michael had not only usurped Ian's holy seat, but had even misappropriated the whole of his former benefactor's outfit. They were in fact his own cap and shirt. Michael's tastes had never been much different from Ian's. And there is nothing particularly original about wearing a baseball cap.

"Hello, Mister Russia," I was greeted, unexpectedly. It was one of those rare occasions when I managed not to be wrong-footed for long. I informed Michael that I had yet to have a sex change and had never been a transvestite. Why then, I asked, should I suddenly be a Mister after all those years of being a maiden. In addition, Russia is feminine in gender, and for good measure I do in fact miss her. Michael accepted my objections and apologized, noting that there was in every woman some-thing of the man (and vice versa). Bill Greenberg chimed in something about women being like countries: Some did not even allow tourist visas, while others issued permanent residence at the drop of a hat, but afterward never let you out. This led to a discussion of the difference between "fatherland" and "motherland." It soon became apparent that Russia was bisexual. It went from Mother Russia to the Soviet Fatherland, and was now becoming Russia again, but of an uncertain sex. Malcolm, sitting next to Greenberg, suggested an alternative: transvestite countries.

I ordered a large whiskey.

"In transvestite countries you can only travel on a transit visa," offered Bill.

"Which country" asked Malcolm, "would you prefer to live in, one with pedophilic tendencies or one with a strong tradition of necrophilia?" completely ignoring Bill. (*Nota bene:* By pedophilic nations, he meant to signify countries that worshiped a cult of youth. America was the prime example of unadulterated pedophilic nationalism. On the other hand, the countries of the East, with their veneration of old age and respect for the authority of the dead, were necrophilic).

"What do you do about Russia?" I queried.

"There are times when a pedophilic state is ruled by a nec-rophile, like America under Reagan..." Greenberg began. Bill was agile in ambivalent situations. He was dressed like a gay disc jockey from a London working-class suburb. In politics he was a latent Bolshevik, though his appearance bespoke a Sex Men-shevik. He ordered another round. I went for another double Grouse.

"Russia is the mirror image of America. That is, a nec-rophilic country ruled by pedophiles," I said, in contribution to Greenberg's geopolitical theory. "Stalin was like a cantankerous child who began a brave new world because his mom and dad had not bought as much ice cream as he wanted. The Peter Pan complex. Arrested development. Michael Jackson's com-plex, too [he was touring Russia at the time]. He wants to stay the same age he was when fame knocked on his door. That's why he seeks the company of young boys," I argued. "He's no different from the exile whose age is forever frozen the moment he leaves his native shores. In his mind, he remains forever young, while his body ages. The picture of Dorian Gray."

"Indeed." Malcolm nodded in agreement. "That's why that infantile freak is always having face-lifts." Michael Wojas then informed us that Jackson had not gone to Russia for a face-lift, but for plastic surgery. He was allegedly preoccupied with a rather different organ of his body. Wojas gave us an earful of rehashed newspaper gossip on the subject. (Barmen have the prerogative of all tyrants to voice aloud whatever tripe may be running through their heads.) As we all knew, the prosecution lawyers demanded photos of his penis—to confirm the exis-tence of its specific features and distinguishing marks. The logic was that if his tool indeed possessed such peculiarities, those little boys who described them had really seen his penis and had therefore been his victims.

At that, Bill Greenberg countered that, even if one of the young bastards had recognized the Jackson willy, it didn't necessarily mean that Jackson had employed it any illicit way. Jackson and the young boys might just have been together in a Russian steam bath. Greenberg said that he himself had been to one, and had found it hard to tell where indecent exposure left off and where the Russian bath began.

"The air is so thick with steam, you can't even tell where your own prick is," he concluded with glum excitement.

"Bad place for Michael Jackson," said Susan. "All the stitches on his face would come apart."

"And his ass with all its face-lifts would just drop off," suggested Big Eddie fancifully.

"Absolutely," said Michael. "Imagine him jumping stark naked into the snow, at minus thirty, after all that heat." Michael shrugged his shoulders Polish-fashion, partly as if trembling from cold, partly to show his spite for such barbaric Russian customs.

"Sounds like Michael Jackson had a good chance of destroying the evidence," giggled Susan.

"Why go so far?" Tom and Steve were puzzled. "Why Russia? Why bother with a bathhouse? Why can't he have plastic surgery at home? He's had his face done there millions of times, so why should his foreskin be any different?"

"While we're on foreskins, circumcision was a precursor to modern plastic surgery. Jews are after all something like white Negroes," said Greenberg.

"Mmm... black man with a white dick—an interesting combination, don't you think?" Malcolm pursed his lips as if in anticipation of something delicious. He ordered another round. The image of a white Negro with facial features that incorporated a displaced foreskin brought smiles on everyone's faces.

Michael saw me smiling and tapped his finger against his frontal teeth, saying,

"Still no plastic surgery, hey?"

He meant the gap between my two teeth. Some people find it charming. The late Ian couldn't let it pass his eye without a vitriolic soliloquy about Miss Russia's ability to perform a blow job without even opening her mouth. To respond to such childish provocation, especially when uttered by a person with a monstrous growth on his face instead of a nose, was beneath me. Besides, the insolence was native to local etiquette. Everyone at the Colony was trapped in an adolescent time warp. That naughtiness helped maintain a distance from the hated world of jumped-up swots, prefects, and ass lickers. As a group, we refused to emigrate into the real world from that lost land. Time either stood still or changed with giant leaps, as happens when death visits your house.

That was when I made that clever remark about Muriel Belcher's nose in Bacon's painting being a prophetic portrait of what would some day happen to Ian Board. The idea was that one person's anatomical features had been reincarnated in another person's body—a man's future embodied in a woman's past. A few of the Christie's people had joined us at the bar. Prompted by the insinuation about the nose in the picture and in real life, Michael recounted once again the circumstances of Ian's demise for the benefit of newcomers. It wasn't a complicated story, considering that for the last twenty or so years Ian had always breakfasted on neat vodka. One can only imagine what his liver looked like. But when Ian got really ill and was taken to the hospital, the doctors said nothing about his liver. He was sent off for an X ray. Lungs was the verdict. Within a week, Ian was dead from a sarcoma, having cursed the doctors during that final interim for their colossal stupidity—that is, their unwillingness to tackle his pickled liver. Liver *schliver* (as Muriel might have said), Ian smoked like a chimney. His horrific throat-clearings, accompanied by coughing fits, could have shaken the bells of St. Martin's-in-the-Fields. Nobody ever objected to his smoking. Who wasn't a smoker? The Colony Room regulars were put on earth to leave behind a gigantic heap of cigarette butts. Ashes to ashes, butts to butts.

"So where's the urn, then?" I asked. His relatives didn't care to accept Ian's ashes. In fact, there was nobody left. Ian had never known his father, his mother was dead, and his brothers had either drunk themselves to death, or ended up in prison or the madhouse. History was repeating itself: Muriel Belcher had run away from her Portuguese Jews, Bacon had fled from his Irish horse breeders, Ian Board had escaped from his debauched half-brethren, and finally, Michael Wojas had run from his Polish Catholics. So, where had Ian's ashes gone? Wojas nodded toward the rows of bottles behind the bar. High above the bar, on the top shelf, was a plaster-of-Paris urn with something written on its side that looked like Japanese.

"Is that it?" I asked. Michael nodded again. His spirit had been laid to rest among those other spirits he spent his life imbibing—inseparable in death as they had been in life.

"With water?" asked Candida (or was it Petronella?), who used to help Michael Wojas behind the bar, and I didn't understand right away what she was asking, so melancholy was the tone of her voice. She was holding a glass of whiskey for me. She did the pouring for Michael, since he had assumed Ian's throne. But the blue-eyed young Candida worked her shifts behind the bar rather irregularly and could never remember who drank what. At the Colony I always feel slightly nervous, hot, and thirsty: I usually have whiskey with a lot of ice and a drop of water. Candida poured water into the whiskey glass from a big carafe. The bar counter is rather high, so she had to jut out her elbow to pour the water, causing her blouse to slip, inviting comparison between her breast's outward contour and the unexposed bit. The gesture was not so much erotic as arrogantly disdainful of the foul-mouthed Soho drinkers with their sex-packed minds ever ready for discharge.

She used to flaunt her artistic ambitions (only appropriate if your name is Candida) and always had a sketch pad ready for the occasional spare moment. She loved to limn the clientele as if they were nude, sometimes as skeletons, or with their bellies ripped open to expose a trail of guts. She (her name was Candida, not Petronella, I now remember clearly) said to me once that the body was only the soul's outer raiment, which she wanted to reveal by stripping away the rotten garment of the flesh. To that end she used to go to anatomy lessons at the medical school where her boyfriend was studying. Her admirers, if she had any, would have pointed out the influence of

Francis Bacon. Anyway, she was listening attentively to what I was saying about the nose in Bacon's painting. She had dreamt of painting a portrait of Ian's nose and secretly sketched it from life when he was too drunk to notice what she was doing. Sometimes he did, though, and then she would be forced to use her sketch pad as a moral umbrella—to protect herself from Ian's downpour of obscenities.

"I wish he could have seen his nose after he died," she sighed romantically, forgetting to put ice in my glass.

"What was there to see?" I asked. "Didn't he ever get a bit fed up with his nose?"

"In death, it changed," she replied enigmatically, knitting her eyebrows in a mental effort to catch something in her mind's eye that the rest of us could not perceive. "Actually, it was the other way round; it turned back into what it had been before we met him." She paused. "You don't believe me, do you?"

"Well, you do get a bit skeptical as you get older," mumbled Michael Wojas.

"I was at his side until the very end," she said with some deliberation. "His heart stopped beating, but I still remained. Everyone left, but I was frozen to the spot. Then I saw it all. His nose began to change."

"What, you mean—disintegrate?"

"No, the opposite!" she said impatiently. "It slowly reverted to its original shape and size. Would you believe it? Began to shrink and lose that horrible purple color. Then it settled, as it were, and gradually turned into just a very ordinary nose. It all happened before my eyes."

We gasped, on the point of giggling, and smiled at each

other idiotically. We didn't know how to react to this revelation. Then everyone fell silent, listening to the street noises of Soho outside the window. A pale ray of light turned into a kind of sunrise on Candida's chin, and her cheeks bore the specterlike reflection of racing green from the walls. All of us there were trying to work out some rational explanation for the mysterious mutations of Ian's nose. The blood must have left it, and the nose assumed its original size—a rotten beetroot no more.

"The miracle lasted a split second," added Candida. "Then he was completely dead," she stammered. "A moment later he looked just like any other corpse, with the nose of any other dead person. But for a couple of seconds before that, his nose was both alive and normal at the same time—an elegant nose, it was, too."

"If the nose was normal, it couldn't have been Ian's," said Michael with an air of authority. He was clearly irritated. An intimate detail of the last minute of Ian Board's life story had been publicly revealed. As the chosen confidant and executor of Ian's will, he should have known about it.

"It was Ian's nose all right—only not the Ian you all knew," Candida shot back. "His nose had returned to its original state, as if he had become young again. Exactly like his earlier photos. Look!" With the same servility as tourists in a coach who follow the instructing finger of a guide, we all swung round to stare at the old snapshots on the wall. "What a pity Ian's spirit couldn't witness this metamorphosis: to come back for a few seconds from the other world and look at the nose of his youth," said Candida, in a somber quavering voice.

"His spirit would have been too drunk to notice the difference," Malcolm ventured. No one smiled. Candida didn't answer. Her chin was trembling. She sniffed and smiled apologetically. I offered her a drink on my tab. She poured herself a "Black Russian," Ian's favorite tipple. She emptied the vodka and Coke in one swig, more or less.

And then she told us Ian's carefully guarded secret, trying to explain how his long-suffering nose had got its grotesque shape. As we listened, I asked myself if it wasn't a bit odd that Ian should tell that girl—a mere passerby in his life—this most intimate story? But then, we often do look for chance encounters to confess our lives' little secrets, like those travelers on long-distance trains in old Russian novels. A handful of gawking London eccentrics, in this godforsaken Soho bar, listened to the simple tale of Candida, as children will listen to a Christmas story.

The story of Ian's colorful nose had a distinct apocryphal tinge to it. Ian had always been regarded as a foul-mouthed celibate, capable only of schoolboy smut, a sexless eunuch. It was like everything on this Prospero's island of ours, only an outward appearance. Muriel Belcher had plucked the young Ian from the gutter. She had taught him the tricks of the trade, and a few circus turns to boot: how to charm the patrons, and how to make obscenity sound like a refined art form. Ian adored Belcher as he had never loved his mother, and treated her with more than filial devotion. But Muriel was a lesbian with strong convictions, and for all her mothering of him, could never let the thought of sex with Ian enter her head. She used to compare the taste of sperm to that of postage stamp glue. And yet she loved Ian rather differently than a foster mother would. Even more so, when her *femme fatale* Carmen left forever.

At this point Candida's rendering of Ian's confessions

began to sound less authentic. Her version of events found Ian and Muriel engaged in a sexual compromise designed to satisfy their mutual hunger for physical intimacy. Penetration was out. Oral sex would be too direct. Candida would thus have us believe that they had settled for nasal sex. That is, Muriel allowed Ian to make love to her with his nose. We all listened to Candida, agape and agog.

Erection (she explained to us patiently as if we were primary school children) occurs when the blood vessels in the male sexual organ swell up with blood. Whenever the insatiable Muriel broke off with her female lover, she would make do with Ian's nose. The more Ian employed his nose as a sexual instrument, the more blood flowed into it, until certain blood vessels filled to the brim. Finally, his nose was in a more or less permanent state of erection. The blood had drained away from his penis and traveled to his nose. It became the indefatigable tool of love's labor, day by day becoming ever more swollen, overworked, overexcited, and bloated with the blood of desire, until his nasal erection was permanently transformed into the monster hooter so familiar to every habitué of Soho.

I watched Michael's face turn ever more gloomy with each word of this obscene and blasphemous chronicle. The bar's regulars stared at Candida as if completely failing to comprehend. When she ended her fantastic story, a deadly silence ensued. For a moment you might have heard the sound of an ice cube melting. Then the bar exploded with laughter. I had not heard the old drunkards laugh so heartily for many a long year. Generally speaking, Greenberg only laughed at his own jokes, and Malcolm's face was only capable of obscene leers. Now all of them were scattered in paroxysms of uncontrolled laughter. Tom and Steve collapsed in a heap with Sarah, Susan, and Big Eddie, in an orgiastic fit of hooting. The lady and gentleman from Christie's smiled anxiously.

How could they know that they were witnessing Ian Board's posthumous triumph? Ian Board after death reached heights he had never dreamed of climbing in life, one that had been remarkable only for its mediocrity, lack of sparkle, and the daily getting up and down from a bar stool. He was never able to forget the golden age of the Colony, when jabbering geniuses elevated all that was sordid and miserable in London life to Olympian dignity and reduced everything highbrow and pretentious to the depths of parody. When wits like Francis Bacon and Jeffrey Bernard were around, Ian skulked in the background, like some gauche youth in the company of his mentors. It dawned on us now that behind the drunken exterior of the barking old grumbler spitting out abusive spleen had been an inspired but clandestine dreamer. He had wanted to get even, and he did it.

Who else but Ian Board could have invented such a macabre tale, claiming it as his most intimate and confidential secret to the most naive and gullible among his chance acquaintances. His cunning was immaculate. With perfect insight, he rightly guessed that Candida would not be able to keep a scurrilous story bottled up and one day would blurt out what a shaming shift he had had to work with his nose. He must have calculated—the old reprobate—that in Candida's childish mouth the story would sound so hilarious that we die-hard cynics would collapse in tears, die laughing. We would raise our glasses to his bright memory and to his macabre sense of humor, with many a toast to his health and well-being—that is, to the hope that he might stay pissed and merry for all eternity.

Still wiping away our tears as the last little spasms died away, we took a fresh look at the old photos of Ian on the walls, with all those legendary transformations of his nose: from its snub turned-up roundness of youth to the infamous spongy splay of later years. The result of love's labor not of disease—that was the gist of its amazing metamorphoses; that was what Ian had meant to convey to us through his bizarre tale. The nose was an artifact of an unmatched passion. Eventually the laughter died away. Candida stood blinking, her arms hanging hopelessly loose, tears welling up in her eyes. It finally dawned on her, no doubt, that the old devil had played a joke on her, and that she had swallowed his story hook, line, and sinker. To break the uneasy silence, Michael started to load the dishwasher in a deliberately noisy manner.

"And what about your own place in eternity? I mean your own survival in the rough world of fine art?" Greenberg asked Candida, almost obsequiously, as if afraid that she would smash her glass into a face that so recently had been contorted with laughter. He was obviously trying to distract her from such thoughts. She shook her head as if waking from a nightmare.

"I'm working on my self-portrait," she replied with half-hidden defiance in her voice, "so I can record the way my nose changes in the future."

"Life size?" asked Greenberg, feigning professional interest.

"Life size," confirmed Candida. "Using natural materials."

"Working in oils, then? Extra virgin?" The usual smirk reappeared on his thick lips.

"In blood, actually," replied Candida. Greenberg choked and dropped his fat cigar into the Bloody Mary before him. The cigar looked like Ian's nose. "My own blood," she elaborated. Then she told us that for several years she had been removing a little blood every day and saving it in the freezer.

"Is that enough?" asked Greenberg, adjusting after the initial shock.

"I can always use my menstrual blood," Candida said, shrugging. Greenberg went paralytic. Even the emotionally indestructible Malcolm showed some revulsion. Candida noticed the involuntary grimace.

"Are you against feminism, or something?" Malcolm emitted angry sounds of protest. Finally, Greenberg's insolent inquisitiveness got the better of his embarrassment, and he said: "Do you use real skin for this self-portrait, too? Where do you take it from?" Then added: "You could always use leftovers from plastic surgery. Say, bits from Michael Jackson and his penis."

"Since you're all so happy, I can add one last detail to the tale of Ian's nose," she said, downing her vodka-and-Coke. "You do know, don't you, that he left his body to the anatomy theater at Barts?" What else should one expect from a militant atheist like Ian? Saint Bartholomew's was also the hospital where her friend, a medical student, took her to sketch during anatomy classes, in the spirit and tradition of Renaissance artists. The morning after Ian's death she had gone there earlier than usual. Having witnessed the phantasmagoric transformations of Ian's nose, she couldn't sleep anyway. Behind its huge doors, the Victorian operating theater was empty. There was the clean dissecting table, where students cut up corpses. All around were formaldehyde tubs where "new arrivals" lay afloat like so many Californian millionaires in their swimming pools. Poor Ian's corpse was lolling there among them.

"I nearly fainted when I saw it," she said.

"Saw what, the nose again?"

"No, not his nose. As I explained, his nose was very elegant," she said impatiently. "I'm not talking about his nose, but his other thing."

"What other thing?"

"The thing at the other end of his body. Opposite end to the nose. His thing, understand? I nearly fainted."

"Which part?"—"What end?"—"Whose thing?"

Candida was barraged with questions from every side of the bar. We all wanted her to pronounce that sacred word.

"Oh come on. You know. Symmetrical to the nose," she mumbled nervously, short of breath, and then blurted it out: "Oh, all right, his penis. His prick, dick, cock, whatever you call it—not so much a penis as a great monster of a thing—huge, purple as a bruise, distended. It was just like his nose, an exact copy of it, in fact. It was as if they swapped places, see." We kept our ears pricked. "As if all the blood had left his nose and gone back to his penis. He must have had a posthumous erection. Only there was nobody there to take advantage of it."

"Yes, pity there are so few necrophiles around," sighed Malcolm.

"I meant Ian was no longer in any condition to enjoy it," Candida blushed.

"That's a totally atheistic statement," said Greenberg. "True, Ian could no longer enjoy his erection in this world. But

27

we don't know what goes on in the other world. That's what eternity is all about, isn't it? Eternal erections?"

"But Ian was a total atheist," said Candida. "So a posthumous erection would have been no use to him either."

"If you don't believe in a thing, it doesn't mean it doesn't happen, does it?" said Greenberg.

"And miracles still happen," said Malcolm. To demonstrate his point he showed everyone that day's issue of the *Evening Standard* with its obligatory Christmas story (from Romania, as it happened). A necrophiliac had broken into a morgue and raped the corpse of young girl. But scarcely had he completed his perverted act when the little girl came round. "She had merely been suffering from, what's it called, lethargy or catalepsy or something like that, and the orgasm brought her round. It was not certain whether he should be jailed or given a prize for restoring the corpse to life. After all, if she hadn't been raped she might have come to in the grave."

The fragmented buzz from the Christmas crowds in the street invaded the silent room for a while and then died away again. The cigarette smoke began to weave Chinese riddles in the thin cold sunlight.

The gothic spell was broken by my old friends Komar and Melamid, Russian conceptual artists from New York. We had been so enthralled listening to Candida that nobody had noticed them appear in the doorway with James Birch. They explained to Candida the trick used by every Russian art student to frighten newcomers to the anatomy theater.

"I am sure students practice the same joke in this country," said Melamid. "Pump formaldehyde into the main vein of a dead man's penis and it stands as tall as a guard in front of

Lenin's Tomb," said Komar. "Or a Beefeater, for that matter," added Melamid. Clearly, Candida had been taken for a ride.

That last callous remark, turning miracle into muck, made Candida feel completely left out. The rest of us, though, sighed with relief. I recalled the stories about spare parts floating in formaldehyde in the room next to the mausoleum, ready to be switched for the worn-out limbs of Lenin's mummy. We all concluded that Damien Hirst, the famous embalmer of greedy sharks and mad cows, could learn a thing or two from the Russians. We forgot about Candida. As the afternoon declined into a winter's evening, we continued pickling ourselves until our entire faces took on the semblance of Ian's nose.

On my way home in the black cab, I chuckled to myself, as I turned it all over in my mind. We stopped at a traffic light. It was as if I were in a bathysphere, suspended in the depths of the giant city, scrutinizing the street life like a deep-sea monster. The whirlpool of neon lights, bright shop windows, and festive crowds, drunk and noisy, looked more dazzling than ever. And I knew the features of this city would forever change, people would come and go, dispensing their funny tricks and bizarre stories, but that I was doomed to remain in the passenger's seat, as if locked in a time capsule, immune to life's trials and tribulations.

The face of a drunk appeared out of nowhere in front of my window. He pressed his big nose against the glass, pulling a moronic face. He was Ian Board, or rather his double, or an apparition. The ghost waved his hand in a farewell and disappeared in the crowd as the taxi moved on.

NO CAUSE FOR ALARM

He used to live in South London, but, being an interpreter by profession, he had to move to the north of the Thames. There were bridges, there were roundabouts, there were streetlights—it was a long journey. The weather was so hot that he had unbuottoned the jacket of his three-piece suit. "Your sort would like it much more over there, sir," said the minicab driver who took him across the river. He kept on expatiating on this point the entire way, eventually concluding that the ambience was more cosmopolitan on the other side of the Thames because people spoke lots of different languages over there (as they were mostly foreigners), "like your sort," the driver elaborated. Noticing Victor's puzzled face in the mirror, he added by way of explanation: "As far as I can judge from your accent, sir." Victor was befuddled by this last remark. He had had his mouth shut the whole time.

Silence speaks with an accent, too. When the driver wasn't talking, he munched bananas nonstop. The floor of his car was strewn with the spotted skins. Victor entertained the thought that this apparent addiction was probably born of the driver's nostalgia for his native banana republic. Bananas gave Victor a nasty heartburn these days, so he envied the driver's addiction, especially since his own nostalgic tendencies more often than not slipped on the banana peel of his memory. Having moved so many times, he no longer could remember anything to be nostalgic about. The driver, catching Victor's curious glance, said apologetically that back in his native land, the government banned the import of foreign bananas with the aim of boosting the consumption of the local variety, which was inedible. Ever since his arrival in England, he regularly sated the gluttonous desire for that forbidden fruit. So much for nostalgia.

Victor was also misled by the driver regarding the cosmopolitan character of his new place of residence. Most of the residents on his street, as Victor quickly discovered, were not multilingual at all. There was certainly no chance of tracing in the local vernacular any word or sound that in any respect echoed his own childhood vocabulary. The new neighbors were, nevertheless, much friendlier and open than those in South London. Indeed, the casual passerby rarely failed to greet Victor, when crossing paths with a whole gamut of welcoming sounds, alternating "hello" and "cheerio," and "hi," and "how d' you do" accompanied by an orchestra conductor's wave of the hand or a wink or a nod or some other gesture aimed to make one feel at home. But he didn't feel at home. He waited patiently, however, as he knew that it takes time to get so used to things that they become invisible—a sensation that for him more or less constituted the feeling of being at home. He was hopeful though: All the signs seemed quite encouraging. He knew he should wait patiently for the day when his neighbors' friendly greetings would reach critical mass, spinning gradually a web of intimacy in which he would be finally trapped—a happy and willing victim.

Nothing of the kind happened.

It would be wrong to conclude that all of the locals kept themselves completely shut off from outsiders. There were some who from time to time invited Victor inside their homes (with the door alarm switched off). They may have talked about excessive sex and violence on the BBC, or perhaps bargain holidays in Turkey and the slump in the property market. He saw that they too had upmarket chain-store furniture; they ate the same sort of food that he did and wore similar clothes. They lived a life very much like his own. He was even presented with a gift of a whistling kettle. There was, however, something about their lives he would never be able to penetrate. Behind their words, gestures, and appearances, there was another life he would never be a part of because of a certain inner deficiency, a hole in his very being that he didn't know how to fill. This gave rise to a sense of shame tinged with guilt; so vague that he had it confused with shyness. The inviting signs and signals others sent to him were like those charming and hypnotizing patterns of hoarfrost on shop windows in winter that obscure the treasures within.

The shop windows on his street attracted Victor with their theatrical beauty, even more than the faces of the smart people who went in and out. The display, say, of kidneys in the butcher's window could compete in sophistication with the jewelry at the boutique on the corner. The grocer's strawberries were in such perfect harmony with the raspberries that together they all seemed as artificial as the toy shop treasures across the street. The marble slabs at the undertaker's showroom were as elegant as the bathroom tiles in the home decorating place next door. The full cycle of human existence was represented by the shops in the street—from the wedding dress shop to the funeral parlor, with the betting shop (brightly painted horses) in between. They were all like still-life studies, mounted, framed, and protected by bulletproof glass. And, mind you, not with glass only. Once when Victor got too close to a beckoning shop window, the burglar alarm went off immediately. The people on the street had a similar trick.

Their polite friendliness obscured their indifference and served the same purpose as a security system. The more attractive the shop window looked, the more sophisticated was the alarm system installed there to protect it. The less responsive people were toward each other, the more sophisticated the alarm system they had equipped themselves with.

Having been unable to penetrate the still-life around him, he began to doubt the wisdom of his move to north of the Thames. He tried to convince himself that nobody in their right mind (or Victor's shoes) would regret the decision to leave South London. His life there had been under constant threat from the intrinsically violent local population. One incident in particular stood out in his memory. Once, on his way home, he popped into The White Elephant (the corner pub) to buy a packet of cigarettes. The machine was broken, so he approached the bar. As the place was overcrowded, he had to get the cigarettes from the barman right over the heads of the regulars, who stuck to the English habit of standing there with their drinks in impenetrable ranks, blocking any access to the bar for newcomers. Victor took it as an affront. As the barman handed over the packet of cigarettes, one of the regulars interfered, insisting that the pub was not an off-license, therefore the packet should be sold, opened, and consumed on the premises. The barman heeded this friendly advice and opened the packet.

"Spare one, mate? Since it's opened anyway," Victor heard the patronizing voice behind his back and immediately somebody's deft fingers snatched a cigarette. Others followed suit. And then another. And another. Victor stood gaping, his mouth mirroring the empty packet in his hand, blinking. He was surrounded by laughing faces. He felt tears about to well up in his eyes. "Smoking damages your health, mate. Cheer up, have a drink," Victor heard, and felt a light, condescending pat on his shoulder. A pint of lager was pushed into his hands. The faces around him, giggling hysterically a moment ago, turned away and resumed their thorough analysis of mad cow disease and recent EEC directives on a more multicultural way of scoring in cricket.

"I should have bought them a round," Victor would repeat to himself each time he recalled the episode, restless and lonely on his North London bed. The teasing memory of that pub encounter would come back to his mind with increasing frequency. The more he dwelt on the humiliating episode, the less humiliating it appeared to him. The humiliation itself, paradoxically, was the only exciting aspect of his otherwise innocuous past existence in South London. Now, the memory of hurtful events made his eventless present feel more drab and dead to him than it had ever been. He did his best, though, to convince himself that the move to North London had been justified. "In a South London pub, people know each other too well and thus make you feel like an outsider. In North London they treat each other like strangers, so you never feel different," he would say to his colleagues during a break, if and when the occasion would arise to express satisfaction with his new place of residence.

North and South London, however, were not terribly different, to judge by Victor's occasional visits to the local pub. He favored The Man in the Moon initially because the walls were all lined with old books. As a translator, he was instinctively drawn to the place as to the library. He was, however, rather disappointed when he picked up a book at random from the shelf and it turned out to be *The Sound Therapy Manual,* published in the last century, half of it in Latin. Other books were of no less obscure a character, written by obscure authors on subjects as obscure as the places where they had been published. The books on these shelves evidently served a purely decorative function. Still, he was bemused by the place, especially by the humorous inscriptions of an aphoristic kind written by the publican in chalk on the blackboard above the bar. The ironic slogans evolved from day to day. For example, "Village Idiot Seeks Village" would become "Village Idiot Seeks Villa." Victor smiled the smile of understanding, as an insider would, when he observed the change upon entering the pub. Understanding—that was what he had been looking for.

He wasn't much of a drinker. On hot summer days he preferred Coca-Cola in those bigger cans, like the ones he saw in American movies. "Large cock, please," he would ask the barman—his accent failing him—and would then slowly comprehend why those nearby split their sides laughing. Otherwise, he was completely ignored by the hard and jolly core of regulars and transients alike. They didn't even think of blocking Victor's approach to the bar, always moving up politely to give way. They didn't desire his company either—this society of men was the epitome of self-sufficiency and self-reliance: Outsiders were tolerated but not welcomed. More and more often, the thought that he had missed his only chance to join the crowd in South London would become unbearably acute. Only one person in the pub gave Victor a glimmer of reason to hope. He looked rather disheveled and uncouth; his balding head and unshaven face resembled a stale half-eaten pita bread with two holes for eyes. His dirty raincoat with a torn shirt underneath was always unbuttoned, a half-empty glass of beer always in his hand. In short, he looked down-and-out. But those eyes of his were constantly shining, he greeted people around him with a friendly wave of the hand and a wink and a smile, and turned his head in different directions, mumbling nonstop with a nod of encouragement or a shrug of contempt in reaction to what he had just heard. Victor secretly gave him the nickname Winky. While others in the pub were stuck in small separate cliques, this jolly gent seemed to be a friend to everyone, as if the whole universe revolved around him as he remained standing in the same spot. He was the only one who never failed to greet Victor each time he entered the pub, and when Victor happened to stand near him, Winky would immediately barrage him with all kinds of opinions on a broad choice of topics, which were difficult for Victor to follow because although he was a translator, Victor couldn't understand a word of it apart from "say no more, mate." But it was encouraging to be welcomed by somebody you had never met before.

The illusion that he was gradually being accepted by the local community was soon to be shattered. It was that spare hour after lunch when Victor had an unexpected break between two assignments. He entered the pub through the side doors so Winky couldn't see him. As usual, Winky stood near the bar nodding, waving to his mates, arguing energetically, and of course winking at somebody Victor couldn't yet see. And then, as Victor approached the bar, it became clear that the place was completely empty. Even the barman had retreated to watch TV. Winky was talking to nobody, mouthing into emptiness. That is, he was talking to himself, not Victor. It dawned on Victor, finally, that this charming Willy Winky was nothing but the local madman, the village idiot. Victor was shocked. To hide his embarrassment, he bought Winky a drink—a gesture that enabled him to pretend that Winky had been talking all this time to him. Victor preferred to be cheated sooner than be disabused.

Victor had grown up in a country where everyone was a part of something greater than his or herself. Some of Victor's compatriots became so closely identified with ideas that were bigger than themselves that their private lives got completely dwarfed by such close proximity, and they had eventually perished. Victor knew better than others how to measure himself cautiously against bigger things, and he survived. But he had suffered too. Nevertheless, the memory of human suffering is short-lived, while the absence of a sense of close proximity to the greatness of human history was, for the likes of Victor, similar to that of an alarm without electricity. In the absence of big issues (in his translation work, he dealt with words, not ideas), Victor was prepared to console himself with the Chekovian notion of "small deeds," such as, for example, helping the elderly. There is only one public place in England where such tasks can be properly addressed: your local library's notice board. But the library's hours kept on changing from week to week, and he was unlucky enough to face a closed door each time he went there. After the last unsuccessful attempt, a schoolgirl offered him her seat on the crowded bus. So he realized that he was not young anymore, and the task of helping the elderly should probably begin at home.

In search of a kindred spirit, he tried, for a change, another establishment in the vicinity called Café Beethoven. But the loud music drowned out any chance for human speech to be heard, and thus for Victor to get involved with the swinging crowd.

Much more unnerving was the wailing and howling of alarms on the street, triggered apparently by the vaguest hint of irregularity or indiscretion on the part of passersby.

Victor wasn't entirely sure whether he was responsible for the abominable disturbance of peace and quiet on the streets. His neighbors did not yet suspect him either. In fact, quite the opposite was true: Since they never took very much notice of Victor, they were more inclined to accuse each other of the crimes against common decency; not bothering to set the alarm correctly or not switching it off in time, and generally abusing civil tolerance. But the fact was that, even with all precautions and care and responsible behavior, the alarms in the neighborhood continued to burst eardrums from dusk to dawn and from dawn to dusk. The police were inundated with complaints. People in the neighborhood began informing on each other. Everyone grew edgy and aggressive. There were all kinds of idiotic conspiracy theories. According to one, the people from the projects nearby were the culprits, which was evident by their criminal disregard for private property, so typical for those who spend their lives on the dole. Some sober-minded citizens of liberal persuasion (of whom there were very few) had to admit gravely that there was a hint of anti-immigrant and racist feelings in the air. The atmosphere of mass hysteria induced in Victor a sense of guilt, and the growing suspicion that it was he, after all, who was the sole perpetrator of the heinous crimes.

This state of self-doubt had some inner resonance, as it were. The more nervous he became, the more he suffered from stomach problems. Two great disorders in his life—the one caused by alarms on the street and the other a long present-issue inside himself—were yet to be linked in his mind. The revelatory connection came about when he was brought on board as interpreter for an international conference on security and crime prevention. As the subject was new to him, he brought brochures, leaflets, and publicity material home in order to study the unfamiliar terminology before the first sessions. The longer he grappled with the exotic vocabulary on the new equipment, the more nervous he became. The sensitivity of some modern alarm systems, he discovered, was mind-boggling. There were contraptions equipped with TV cameras to set an alarm off if the person who tried to open the door was of the wrong appearance (his nose was too long, say); there were sensitive devices that could detect an unusual walking pace, the wrong color eyes, and others that could distinguish between different body odors. All these sophisticated systems did, of course, automatically recognize the owner's pitch of voice, and reacted alarmingly to any alien utterance.

It was this last specification of the alarm system equipment that made Victor realize the unpleasant truth. These days his stomach was worse than ever. His belly rumbled loudly, sometimes playing the flute, sometimes hissing like an old record player. It was all rather upsetting. Just before Easter that year it was quite hot, and his apartment, stuffed with dictionaries and thesauruses, was both cramped and stifling. In the evenings Victor would go out for a stroll, to memorize new terminology while walking along the street. The shops were shut, the alarms set. The revelation occurred as Victor was idly surveying the shop window of the local undertaker, now advertising a new way to make your love and memory of the deceased eternal by having a signature, or any other manifestation of identity, engraved on a tombstone. While he was still trying to penetrate the profound implication of the undertaker's suggestion, his stomach produced a sound resembling an avalanche of tombstones on Judgment Day. Immediately, the undertaker's alarm started to scream like the legions of the resurrected.

Bewildered and frightened, Victor scuttled away from the scene of the crime to hide in his room. The street he left behind was in turmoil. Most of the shop alarms had gone berserk, and were joined by rows of car alarms. As it happened to be a weekend, few shop owners were around to have the alarms switched off. People were hanging out windows, accusing and cursing each other, demanding that an end be put to this latest outrage. A newly formed group of vigilantes gathered in front of the local pub across the street to discuss the possibility of a house-to-house search for the culprits. Victor was poised by his window, furtively watching this search for the mysterious noisemaker. He was somewhat enthralled by his own mischief. He now understood the terrorist's angst—that longing for recognition from the indifferent crowd, the yearning to be incorporated into a larger emotional entity, to engrave one's immortal signature on the tombstone of public life. Unlike the terrorist, though, Victor's misdeeds were not of his own volition. They traveled through him, via his guts, as an act of God. He had an urge to go out, to join the crowd, to witness the anger, the obverse side of the rapture and elation accompanied by a manifestation of God. Victor knew he was an instrument of that power.

Victor had before experienced such emotions only during occasional visits to the opera house in Covent Garden. He used to buy the cheapest tickets in the top rows of the amphitheater, right under the ceiling, and sit there, glued to his seat, absolutely entranced by the onslaught of mighty sound that in one almighty embrace transported the audience, and characters on the stage, to unreachable heights before tossing them back to the ground, crushing them on the misery of earthly existence, making them burst into an unbearable tremolo of despair. Victor, looking like a Gogolesque clerk, would sit there petrified, his facial muscles conducting a string orchestra—a disconcerting sight for those next to him in the audience. Ever since his stomach had started to play its own tunes, he had been forced to discontinue these visits to the opera. His window was now his theater stall, and the passersby down in the street his operatic characters. Materialistic as they were, his neighbors were so preoccupied with the search for the outward cause of their distress to ever suspect the intestines next door. Days passed; Victor's stomach kept setting off the alarms, and his growing sense of impunity allowed him to feel less than threatened.

Only one person in the area made him fear exposure. She lived nearby. Whenever she saw him hurrying furtively down the street, she followed his steps with a watchful eye. He always tried to get out of her sight as soon as possible. Victor reckoned there was something more malicious in her unwelcome gaze than the mere suspicion of an outsider. Her looks, incidentally, were not unpleasant but were somewhat lacking the feminine touch. Though well proportioned, her big-boned body was both large and tall, with broad manly shoulders, and closely cropped rye-yellow hair. Always neatly dressed, she looked the paragon of modesty, discipline, and diligence. Victor had seen her in the pub a few times, selling prawns from a basket; she also worked occasionally in the kitchen of a local vegetarian restaurant. Once he noticed her cleaning windows, and he'd also seen her taking a group of toddlers for a walk in the park. She earned her crust it seemed, in the hardest, most direct way, without looking for excuses and allowances because of her sex, origins, or worldviews. She was, in short, a walking symbol of hard-working, self-effacing, suffering-in-silence England, while he, Victor-the-menace, was a smart foreigner bastard engaged in rather dubious activities, polluting the atmosphere with the noise of inner resentment.

It was not hard to guess what sort of image Victor might have cast on her eyes in the early morning hours as she went off to perform her manual jobs, while he, who worked strange shifts as a translator, headed home dressed like a rake on the razzle, in a state of inebriation after a night of interpreting for dignitaries during some ceremonial banquet or late-night private party. He felt her spite each time they met, although she never uttered a sound of disapproval. She was in fact the only one who never pretended to like him. Passing him by, she would hardly raise her eyes to acknowledge his clumsy attempts at an ingratiating bow. However, once she passed, Victor would feel her penetrating stare trained on his back. He tried to remain calm, repeating to himself reassuringly that she couldn't possibly have identified him as the main cause of the disturbances on the street. There was no cause for alarm. Yet, one had to be on constant alert when confronted with eyes such as hers.

During acute moments of panic Victor always went to the local pub. He decided that his noisy persona might become invisible amid the general noise; he also drew some pleasurable excitement from witnessing his contribution to the life of society, enchanted by the effect his mischievous deeds had on his fellow human beings. For this purpose—to give the impression that he was mingling with the rest—he would sit at the bar next to mad Winky, who kept on talking and gesticulating to everyone in the pub and, at the same time, to no one in particular. Victor, per usual, felt less excluded when he sat with Winky. Personal security apart, it was intrinsic to Victor's nature to impress others as being an amiable and gregarious chap. One evening, a few weeks after he had discovered the provocative aural powers of his stomach, he was standing there next to Winky when his belly burst into a trumpet solo that would have made Miles Davis jealous. To the crowd of philistines congregating in the pub, this little horn solo might have been easily confused either with a car horn or with the sound—whose peculiarity depends on the publican's whim—with which the end of drinking hours is announced. Nobody would have paid much attention to that strange squeak had it not been echoed by the alarms on the street, which simultaneously started to ululate madly, one after another. Everyone in the pub began shouting and swearing and cursing, condemning the cretins, mouthing solemn oaths to find and castrate the bloody bastards. Still, nobody had made the connection between the strange sound emitted by Victor's innards and the screaming of the alarms outside.

Nobody, that is, except for the local idiot, Winky, who stood next to Victor. He stopped his rigmarole of winks, nods, and natter, and stared at Victor. An unpleasant smile of comprehension distorted the weak mouth of that unholy fool. In his twinkling eyes Victor suddenly detected for the first time clear signs of intelligence. Victor quickly moved away from Winky to join the crowd and contribute his portion to the general outburst of hatred, cursing, swearing, and shouting with the others.

It was too late, though. Victor saw Winky approaching one

of the regulars, then another, leaning over their shoulders, whispering something into their ears. "Judas," Victor muttered to himself, as he watched his supposed friend—the one who not long ago had been the only flimsy evidence to sustain Victor's faith in the brotherhood of men—utterly betray him. Neither the vigilantes nor the regulars could comprehend what Winky was trying to convey to them. They shrugged their shoulders in disbelief; some turned their heads away; some giggled hysterically. But the longer Winky insisted, the more visibly their mood changed. Soon there were suspicious glances toward the corner where Victor stood. He could no longer restrain the fear that crept up his spine and, without further ado, made for the door. They rushed after him—all of the them—as if waiting for the signal. The last thing he saw as he glanced back through the pub doors was Winky, who was finishing off in fast succession the half-empty beer glasses left behind on the tables.

Running down the street, with a crowd at his heels, Victor panted heavily, his stomach chased by the ever-growing howl of alarms. This is the end, Victor thought. After the incident in the South London pub many years before, when he had come face-to-face with an aggressive crowd, he hoped never to experience the fear of an intimidating mob again. He remembered his nostalgic longing for the confrontation that might provide him with a chance to become a part of communal life. This time he even thought of turning back—to face those who chased him, to confess his mischief, to laugh it off, and to embrace his new friends who would be only too glad to accept such an honest and jolly fellow into their midst. He stopped for a fraction of a second and immediately realized how futile were his hopes for reconciliation with the world: The small gang that had started to chase after him in the pub had now been joined by passersby. They craved his blood.

There are many reasons for moving from one place to another. Rational explanations of something as irrational as emigration change with hindsight, as life goes on and our perception of the past changes along with it. There is still a sterling standard to measure the wisdom of that kind of foolish act. It is called fear. Until the very moment he was exposed in the pub, Victor had been convinced there was nothing to fear while he remained to the north of the river. Chased by a crowd consisting of liberal intelligentsia and the chattering underclasses, joined by the family of the undertaker, a delivery boy from a Pakistani minimarket, and many others, Victor was brutally disabused of any illusions. The fear was exactly the same as it had been south of the Thames. Modern life follows the same recipe as well-written verse (as prescribed by "The Waste Land"): Life shuns the echoing of events in the same way that modern poetry shuns rhyme—rhyme heralds the end of life's poesy.

"This is the end," Victor now muttered aloud as he saw himself gradually encircled by angry faces seeking vengeance and justice. But he was mistaken: It was yet another beginning. He turned into a small lane that looked like a dead end, but Victor knew that between a huge chestnut tree and the garden wall there was a narrow passage that led, after a sharp turn, into an adjacent street. That was an obvious route for escape had it not been for a tall woman standing between the tree and the wall. The setting sun burst through the crown of the chestnut, blinding Victor as if it were a police searchlight. The light formed a nimbus around the woman's head, darkening her face.

But Victor recognized her immediately, her cropped hair, her broad shoulders and ample belly. She stood there triumphantly waiting for the quarry to fall into her trap. She was leaning on the gate in the garden wall, which she kept ajar like a trapdoor. Victor stalled for a moment, panting, his eyes blinking, mouth open. The bloodthirsty mob was about to appear from around the corner. Since he couldn't disappear into thin air, he lunged through the open gate. The gate shut behind him with a bang. Victor was ready to bounce back belligerently as he felt the woman's heavy hand on his shoulder. But she put her finger against his lips. There was a wall behind him. The garden before him was an intricate maze of trees and bushes. He stepped cautiously inside, intrigued and bewildered. He fainted.

She put him up for the night in a strange hut in the garden, which was more like a workshop than a garden shed. It was packed with a bizarre assortment of recording equipment, microphones of various types and sizes, along with other contraptions that purred, hissed, and clicked unobtrusively as if whispering their impressions of the new lodger. He peeped outside. The garden walls were very high and very thick, so every sound inside and outside the house resonated against them, filling the garden with the chirping of birds, cooing pigeons, the swish of a squirrel's tail in the chestnut, and the rustle of a hedgehog in the bushes. Victor was astounded to find that while living in his apartment on the top floor facing High Street, he had completely forgotten the sight and sound of garden life. As he viewed the yellow windows of nearby houses glowing in the darkness, he came to the conclusion that he had seen this garden before, from his bathroom window, often admiring the beauty of that verdant enclosure more intensely indeed than its rightful owner because he, Victor, wasn't responsible for its care and preservation. He loved this garden vicariously, watching others cultivating it to perfection. While it is beyond certification that we grow uglier with every season, the garden preserves its eternal charm; the English love of gardens is thus another manifestation of their masochistic nature. Victor preferred to think of himself as standing apart from the English nation, but inside the English garden. There was, no doubt, an inconsistency here. He felt the self-contradictory nature of his stance more acutely than ever because this time he had no choice but to stay with his asylum keeper, inside the garden. He watched how the tops of the trees moved with the wind against a sky in which clouds moved even faster. The sky and the trees were in motion without moving. It dawned on Victor suddenly that his life had changed irreversibly without the aid of emigration or river crossing.

When night fell, she came to the shed, got into his bed, climbed on top of him, and fucked him in a deliberate and diligent fashion. She had a big, round, and very firm belly, like one of those copper cauldrons in which the Swiss cook cheese fondue. While screwing him, she rotated her hindquarters rhythmically, and her belly rotated accordingly, pressing Victor's stomach in a regular circular movement, counterclockwise. His stomach responded to the pressure with the most bizarre sounds ever to have been emitted by the human bowels. These queer sounds didn't disturb her in the least. The opposite was true: The more audible their intercourse became, the more precise the choreography of her belly dancing. Having reached orgasm simultaneously, he blasted with a fart, and she triumphantly burst into the operatic aria *"Nessun Dorma."*

Indeed, if any people were still asleep in the area, they would have been roused immediately by the alarms on the street, which burst into action as if booing their performance. Only the recording equipment purred approvingly in the darkness, clicking and whirring softly as if expressing their contentment and satisfaction with what they'd just heard. The variety of equipment in the shed remained a mystery to Victor, but the twinkling and winking of the panels created in him a sense of security, as if safeguarding him from the cruel noise of the outside world. As soon as their sexual encounter was over, she leaned over him with her face pressed against his belly, as if listening, like a pediatrician with her ear at a child's tummy, to the silence restored inside his bowels. Victor had noticed how delicately her ears were formed. They had no earlobes and grew straight out of her head like a cat. They were, she assured Victor, perfectly tuned to detect the finest variations of a stomach's rumblings. She had inherited that gift from her father.

Wanda, or Wonderwoman (Victor's secret nickname for her), told him that the moment she met him on the street she had known about Victor's abdominal peculiarities. Her late father, she explained, suffered all his life from the same complaint until he married Wanda's mother, who had managed to keep this illness at bay, though not without a prolonged struggle. Wanda's mother had passed her knowledge on to her. According to her arcane teachings, the rumbling was caused by the dysfunction of a tiny muscle that regulates the opening between the stomach and the gullet. When that "inner muscle" becomes weak, air which has accumulated in the bowels bursts through the gullet in a somewhat forceful and chaotic fashion, producing those bizarre noises that tripped the alarms on the street. Wanda was nostalgic, hearing once again the magic sound of a roaring stomach, like her late father's. According to Wanda's mother, the cure came from a unique combination of intense sex and a careful diet. The afflicted person should eat foods that make the "inner muscle" really work—namely, all kinds of beans: green beans, black beans, mushy peas, lentils yellow and green, and similar stuff, while the belly muscles were to be exercised by the persistent rotating movements of the healer's pelvis. Wanda and Victor became engaged in the repetition of that treatment many times a night, and sometimes during the day too. Victor couldn't believe that the person whom he used to regard as a threat to his existence a short while ago had now become the instrument of his salvation.

But Wonderwoman was not only motivated by her commiseration with human suffering and compassion for the underdogs of society. Her father, Swiss by birth, had been an amateur composer of conceptual music, and Wanda had followed in his footsteps. In keeping with the old British tradition of an amateurism in the arts, she followed in her father's footsteps, toiling all day, earning her living by manual jobs, while indulging herself at night in the creation of the most wild and daring forms of modern music. Her father had worked his entire adult life on a symphony of Swiss cowbells. But so horrendous had been his rumblings that he went partially deaf, thus preventing the completion of his life's masterpiece. With the pathetic antediluvian equipment at his disposal, he had still managed to record hours and hours of the cowbell's ting-a-ling amid the meadows in the Swiss Alps. He believed that the movement of grazing cattle created a definite pattern. It emerged only after days, maybe months, of following the cattle. It corresponded in part to the meadows in which they grazed, and partly to the movements of the grazing bull, which were repeated by the rest of the herd. If such a pattern is discernible in cattle movements, then the jingling cowbells, he surmised, would have a corresponding pattern. Wanda's father spent his last days with headphones glued to his head, listening to miles and miles of cowbell tape. In the end, he failed to create any semblance of symphonic structure from the hidden pattern of cow movements. His ears were simply too warped by the sound of his stomach.

In the course of her own creative efforts, Wonderwoman made another logical step forward, far beyond her father's musical ambitions. She decided to incorporate all effects of audible interference, every last decibel of ambient noise, in the recording. What had prevented Wanda's father from completing the symphony was to become a part of hers. Her symphony would follow Victor's stomach rumblings, punctuated with her moaning during their therapeutic sexual communion, set against the background of the car and shop alarms. It was a symbolic juxtaposition of inner and outward freedom. In her grand musical design, Wanda had boldly transformed her father's cowbells into the alarm bells of that sacred cow of Western civilization—private property. The symphony was to be called "No Cause for Alarm."

Wanda believed in the healing power of sound, so the symphony was to have its first public performance among her fellow believers at a forthcoming New Age Convention. Composing the symphony had been a protracted, complicated, and exhausting process of fucking, recording, dubbing, editing, splicing, fucking again, and other mysterious operations that Wanda performed on the tapes until the small hours of the night. While Wanda hardly ever ceased working on the symphony, Victor had to sleep wearing earplugs to muffle the recorded borborygmi and alarms. Meanwhile, the original source of Wanda's creation was growing calmer day by day. He became more serene, wandering absentmindedly around the apartment, doing little to nothing with his days. He stopped checking the calendar and could no longer be entirely sure how many months had passed since he found refuge with Wanda.

One day he woke up to find himself alone in the house. Wanda often left early to do her various jobs. But in the shed he found a note. She had gone to attend the first public performance of her symphony at the Cambridge Festival and would be there for some time. Then followed instructions as to where to find the baked beans and other canned goods (on the bottom shelf in the cupboard under the sink) so that he wouldn't starve while she was away. Victor had breakfast, then lunch, then an evening meal on his own, and only when it was time for his therapeutic sex did the terrible void in his existence become apparent. Having given some consideration to this feeling he became aware of the surrounding silence. His stomach had been still all day long. There was an unusual silence outside his body as well; no hint in the air of any alarms—the street was deadly calm.

When he finally plucked up courage and ventured out—glancing around furtively before stepping cautiously outside the front door—he found the street pretty much unchanged, although spiritually it was drastically transformed. There was no festive bustle of sharply dressed people smiling and talking to each other. Apart from a lone drunkard staggering toward the pub, the street was empty, sidewalks strewn with trash, shops protected by metal gates. The butcher and the bridal shop, as well as the old hairdresser's salon, had disappeared. They had been replaced by enigmatic establishments whose names were difficult to read behind the metal bars. Only the undertaker had survived the change and still displayed behind barless plate glass the advertisement about making your "last one" immortal. The shop was closed, though, and Victor noticed an impressive solid alarm bell had been installed by the corner of the window. He noticed similar equipment at a number of shops. In the past, residents and shopkeepers had not flaunted their alarm systems. The new owners and dwellers made it clear that they were heavily guarded. The most dramatic difference was that these alarms were silent.

Victor was attracted by the din of voices behind the pub doors. He recoiled into a corner the moment he entered the room in reaction to the welcoming gesticulations from the same village idiot, Winky, who had once so treacherously set the lynch mob on him. He had hardly changed. Madness is timeless. Victor got a hold of himself; he remembered that Winky's gesticulation was not directed at anyone in particular; he had not recognized Victor. But he was talkative all the same, and his prattling, incomprehensible as ever, helped Victor to feel more at ease. He started talking to the new publican, a gentleman of the same swarthy appearance as his many new customers. The publican and many others talked to Victor with pleasure, explaining with some relish the past history of the area.

According to them, a few years ago there lived in the area a breed of rather haughty, irritable people who had these alarm systems attached to shops, houses, and cars that were set to go off for no reason other than to warn off potential robbers. The total lack of consideration and utter disregard for the peace and comfort of others reached such proportions that the police stopped paying any attention to the alarms. The situation was exploited by professional burglars, who knew that no one was taking an alarm seriously when it went off. They went about stripping the area of its valuables systematically, house by house, shop by shop. Residents began to sell their houses and businesses. In their stead, more enterprising though dubious traders and businessmen moved into the abandoned premises. The local council had managed to buy houses from anxious owners at hardly any expense, and they were converted into public housing for the poor and needy.

The local population had changed beyond recognition. From dawn to dusk the unemployed social misfits, sex deviants, and ethnic minorities shuttled up and down the street from the pub to the DHSS office and back, and then to their council estates for a nightly snore so they could be back on the same route the morning after. They were inward-looking people who were indifferent to popular opinion and were consequently lackadaisical about their own appearances, an attitude which extended to the maintenance of public spaces. There were a lot of banana peels, for example, which posed a lethal risk for pedestrians. This fact was totally disregarded by the street sweepers and trash collectors. Their dirty ugly trucks, like prehistoric monsters, would whip up the dust instead of sweeping it, and scattered the trash far and wide, leaving more than they collected while emptying the bins. The local buses didn't always stop, and the local school resembled a prison with its brick walls and barbed wire. The local boys were known to pollute the air with foul language of such intensity that it seemed a cloud of swear words hung over the walls like those thick artificial penises at any one of several neighborhood porn shops.

To Victor's paranoid mind, this was part of a well-thought-out strategy. It was the local council who ruled supreme in this universe, like a father over his retarded children. "Yob" was nothing but the reverse of "boy." The longer Victor the wise-man studied the situation, the more he became convinced beyond any doubt of a conspiracy; the local councilors were deliberately encouraging deprivation and dereliction in the area: The poorer the population became, the more dependent people were on the help and care provided by local councilors, so the stronger was their tendency to vote for the party with a majority on the council. "These socialist bastards should be castrated and thrown into the dustbin of history," mumbled Victor, swearing at what he saw. Then he remembered that the dustmen were on strike and the bins would probably be left unemptied till the next generation of councilors.

Although he too was unemployed, he didn't see himself as one of this crowd. They were slobs and yobs, scavengers who deliberately sponged off hard working people who duly paid their taxes, while Victor was out of a job because of his forced disappearance from the real world in Wonderwoman's house. It was not his fault. Wanda was to blame for his current misery. Had it not been for her sophisticated sexual tricks to which he had become so addicted, and for her obsessiveness with his infirmity—which she had ruthlessly abused and exploited to fulfill her perverse musical ambitions—Victor would have slipped away from her house under cover of the night immediately following his lucky escape from the lynch mob. He would have moved back to South London, where nobody suspected his peculiarities and the alarms were not as sensitive as they were on this side of the Thames. He would once again lead the life of an ordinary translator.

This and many other opportunities in life were now lost forever. Even his freakish rumblings had become part of somebody else's symphony. Indeed, no week passed without this or that newspaper carrying a piece on the extraordinary creative power of the newly emerged genius of British music who managed to weld together the mystical vocal energy of Eastern inner wisdom and the mechanical harshness of Western civilization. Mystical vocal energy, indeed. Victor was indignant. His stomach was silent as he read that piece of gibberish in the paper. Every puff of the mystical energy he ever had in his entrails had been absorbed by her symphonic blather, which, since Cambridge the previous year, had been heard in every corner of the world, to judge by the newspaper reviews and Wanda's occasional postcards from around the globe. Rage welled up in Victor's head: He had been robbed of his very essence and there was no alarm to alert mankind to the heinous dispossession Wanda had caused. He no longer even felt like visiting the opera house.

Now and here added up to nowhere for Victor. Life in transit made him a victim of circumstance. He did not belong to himself; everything that he had said and done belonged to somebody else.

Many months passed with Victor in limbo. One quiet summer afternoon he was sitting with a beer glass at a table outside his local, among unshaven and unkempt faces, young and old, discussing fiscal changes in the social security benefits and the notion of the relativity of causes and consequences, when suddenly she was there. She had just turned the corner at the far end of the street when he saw her walking toward the pub in a black silky outfit that made her tall and corpulent figure seem sprightly and elegant. The silk clung to her body tightly enough to outline her well-formed belly that moved with her thighs. He'd forgotten how considerable in size and how refined her features were. She was so large and beautiful, any show of envy or resentment toward her was dwarfed. Victor felt a sudden upsurge of nostalgic longing for their mutual past when they both were involved in the creation of something complex, big, and beautiful. It almost seemed that the time he had spent with her was the closest he had come to living an ideal. For the briefest moment, he had really belonged to something bigger than himself. Her cropped hair and strong features made him feel repentant, and the tears started to well. He longed to touch her cute cat's ears, but they were covered by earphones.

Victor had immediately guessed what she was listening to. The moment Wonderwoman hit the High Street, an alarm went howling mad. One outburst was followed by another, and soon the whole street was drowned in hysterical wailing. The crowd of drinkers and passersby were irritable, swearing and shouting. The old fear of an anarchic mob running after him made him edgy. He had no intention of facing that again. He had to stop the noise; he had to stop that woman with her recordings of a dreaded past, which cost him such effort to overcome and forget.

"That old bitch and her idiotic recordings," he muttered to himself but immediately realized that he had been overheard. His neighbors at the table turned to him: "Which recordings? Who are you talking about?" They followed his gaze, fixed on Wanda as she approached the pub. The rumor as to who was the real perpetrator of the havoc on the street quickly spread. The few brave souls from the crowd encircled Wanda and demanded that she hand over the tape recorder. She bluntly refused to do so. The circle of angry faces narrowed around her. One hand stretched forward, trying to snatch her Walkman. Another hand pulled at the sleeve of her frock. The sound of slaps and blows reached Victor's ear as Wanda disappeared behind the backs of the mob.

Victor watched from a distance as the crowd around Wanda grew larger and larger. The confrontation was flaring up. Suddenly, a screech pierced Victor's ears; he recognized Wanda's voice, but the pitch of it was bizarre—a harsh and squeaky cry of pain, not the familiar velvety soprano that accompanied their lovemaking. Victor watched the Walkman get thrown to the ground and crushed under someone's Doc Martens' heel. For a fraction of a second he glimpsed a bleeding face next to the smashed recorder—the face of Wonderwoman. The wailing of the burglar alarms was joined by police sirens and an ambulance. As soon as the crowd dispersed, Victor moved forward. Wanda was already on the stretcher about to be carried to the ambulance. Their eyes met for a fraction of a second and he read there astonishment, rather than reproach. It was clear that she would not make it to the hospital alive.

Once the place was cleared and the alarms switched off, Victor returned to the pub and had a stiff one. Slightly tipsy, he played for a while with the notion of claiming authorship of the havoc provoked by the recording of his yesteryear stomach problem. He was prudent enough, however, to suppress the promptings of his vanity. He felt his pride satisfied at least with the fact that, with the accidental death of his coauthor, no one in the universe other than himself could identify the origins of the bizarre symphonies once ascribed exclusively to that big, broken woman. He removed the cassette from Wanda's shattered Walkman and slipped it into his pocket. He burned it in the garden near the shed.

Since he was now the sole occupier of the garden apartment that had belonged to the late Wanda, the framework of his mind and social temperament went through a considerable transformation. He deemed it frivolous, even dishonest, to criticize the current state of affairs in the area without making the attempt at changing it. He began campaigning for active participation in community life. As he knew many languages and had a swarthy face not so very different from many of those who populated that part of town, he soon became irreplaceable in dealings between residents and the local authorities. There was always the need for an interpreter who could sort out the variously obscure positions held by the locals. He had only to change his occupational specifications slightly to fit the task.

His future was bright. As unlikely as it may seem, Victor

was a natural politician. He was instrumental in the local effort to lift parking restrictions, which were bringing a buccaneer's profit to the local authorities but hurt local businesses. Victor would go on from there to far more momentous issues. Privatization of waste removal. Victor was a champion of the streets. He believed that privatization would make everyone infinitely more conscientious than they had ever been. He was right. It was just a matter of time before Victor became a member of the local council.

And so it came to pass that Victor found his calling in garbage. But the most winning moment in Victor's career was yet to come.

Near the main lights on the High Street the newly challenged sanitation department had put out special receptacles for green glass bottles, brown glass bottles, and clear glass bottles. There was a separate place for Oxfam books, which excluded old editions of the *Encyclopedia Britannica,* and another bin was allocated for clothing. There was also a receptacle for newspapers, but not the same one which served for telephone directories, which, in turn, warned citizens not to drop in used writing paper, which had better not be confused with toilet paper rolls. Soon after the establishment of this miniature town of trash containers, Victor saw an old lady with a number of carrier bags, standing there as if she faced the Egyptian pyramids. Victor, his heart bleeding for the helpless lady, watched silently how, completely defeated by this multiple choice of receptacles, she emptied all her bags on the sidewalk, already strewn with litter.

Tears welled up in Victor's eyes as he watched the despair of this simple hardworking woman, humiliated by the sophistry of social demagoguery. Who could deny that this was a mere environmentalist ploy aimed to please the sanitation workers? They would never again have to sort out the different kinds of refuse themselves. From that moment on, already a keen garbage advocate, Victor pledged to ceaselessly defend his part of town from the encroachment of the enemies of the people.

As a result of this and many other revelatory exposures, the opposition headed by Victor became a power to reckon with. Real change had begun to affect the area. The riffraff element that used to dominate the place started to feel out of place. They slowly began to abandon that part of town. These vacated spots were adopted by a decent lot, people with money and a sense of civic duty. The area was gradually restored to its former glory.

One morning Victor woke up with a strange premonition niggling at his heart. After a hard but productive day in the office, where he was chairing a number of committees, he took a stroll in the park, enjoying the sunset. On his way home, Victor proudly observed the range of improvements that had been introduced locally through his good offices and initiative. The houses and shops had bright, freshly painted facades with windows that looked like still-lifes in a museum. Solemn tranquility ruled over this world of prosperity, family ties, and community bonds. There was a place for everyone, and everyone was in his place. The street was drowned blissfully in the golden evening haze.

Suddenly Victor saw him: a lonely, outlandish-looking gentleman cautiously negotiating his way between the stalls of the local vegetable market. With a battered suitcase in hand, threadbare three-piece suit unbuttoned because of the evening heat, he was out of keeping with the serenity of the street. Passing him, Victor deliberately slowed his steps and nodded in a friendly way, as he mumbled a greeting, smiling openly to reassure the stranger that he was welcome here. Victor then ran toward his house. Before shutting the gate, he threw back a surreptitious glance. He saw the pathetic figure standing in the middle of the street, wiping the sweat off his forehead, then, absentmindedly stooping to peer at the one of the many beautiful shop windows. A shudder seized Victor's body. He didn't want to know what would happen next. Trembling, he rushed inside and bolted the doors behind him.

That night he went to bed earlier than usual and fell fast asleep. He dreamt he was being taken back to South London by minicab. "Your sort will like it better over there "cause it's more cosmopolitan," the driver said. Victor couldn't see his face.

He woke up in the darkness, sweating. The wailing of alarms raged outside throughout that long night. He remembered the uncompromising God of the Hebrews who takes away from man everything that belongs to him, in order to guide him back where he belongs.

DOUBLE ACT IN SOHO

The encounter occurred during that happy era when small businessmen were feverishly discussing joint ventures and the illusory millions that were supposedly up for grabs in Perestroika Moscow. The Iron Curtain was becoming increasingly moth-eaten. But for the émigrés of the seventies, the idea of quitting London for Moscow was unthinkable. In their minds London was still the romantic ideal—ever enchanting, mysterious, and unfathomable.

After twenty-five years in voluntary exile, I can tell you with the whole authority of a professional that each and every émigré is not only a secret Columbus in his very own America, but also the tyrant-king of whatever nation he alone has discovered. He's like a savage child who has touched something, given it a name, and henceforth regards it as his personal property. The charm of this absolute monarchy is that it exists only in the mind of the monarch himself, and he has no need to share with anyone. The actual indigenous population—its people, its rulers and its parliament—represent no threat whatever to this monarchical bent. They are merely stage props required to maintain a necessary illusion. A threat can arise from one direction only—when a foreigner makes an appearance on the tyrant-king's territory, another lost soul like himself from the same motherland (or even worse, from the same city), who surveys the land and sets about rediscovering and restyling it after his or her own fashion.

Perhaps this is why I could so easily empathize with Alec's anxiety (I saw him occasionally, a middle-aged wreck of émigré life, during my visits to the BBC Russian Service), when his ear detected the Russian accent in the din and noise of the pub. This was the human footprint in the sand of his previously uninhabited island. Of course, on an uninhabited island, a fellow human being might prove to be the very cannibal who would devour you.

Perhaps I romanticize the tension in the air, the awkwardness of the encounter. In any case, I have no doubt that the appearance of another Russian face among the regulars at The French House had the power to strip him of the special status he enjoyed as the Russian Emperor of London. Alec was flattered whenever the publican Gaston Berlemont nodded to him just as benevolently as he did to some celebrity like Francis Bacon. Be accepted by this crowd and you might soon be rubbing shoulders with the choice derelicts of The Colony Room or the thespian decadents of Gerry's Club down the street. (I belong to both.) The squalid interior of this legendary venue suited Alec very well, with its scuffed oak paneling, its tobacco-colored stucco ceiling, its worn, butt-littered linoleum, and the mishmash of cheaply framed photographs that documented the pub's history, which had no aristocratic or imperial pretensions to threaten or intimidate. It was a history foreign to him, of course, but now no longer alien; it was a history created during his own lifetime, in which (at least in principle) a place could have been found for him, if only he'd been born *here* instead of *there*.

Alec rightly felt this female stranger was trespassing. These "New Russians" arrive in London as gawking tourists to gape at others and show themselves off; they buy a stereo for a relative back home and CDs for someone else, and then, before they've been in London any time at all, you will hear them bombarding everyone with their opinions about the British way of life, its legends and myths. They rob a person like Alec of his cultural crust, all his little discoveries—for instance, the fact that the word "exiles" is identical with "ex-isles," defining those who live outside: off the British Isles. It was *his* London, his and nobody else's. His Big Ben. His Buckingham Palace. His Tower of London and his British Museum. His Soho. Even the sex shops were his, regardless of the fact that he'd never been in one. Alec grimaced as he took a swig of his whiskey, and then immediately hid behind his newspaper because it seemed to him that she might have caught a glimpse of his ugly face staring at her.

The newspaper hid his face almost entirely, like a yashmak long overdue for the laundry. His eyes seemed to be lowered as modestly as though looking at the newspaper, but in actual fact they were slyly darting to and fro. Or in actual fact, not simply to and fro, for his eyes constantly returned to one and the same face in the crowd. He watched with half an eye as the line of her bangs rose and fell in the throng of heads and shoulders as she turned to her next partner in conversation. Admirer? Lover? Every now and then her bare arm reached out toward the bar for her kir, with the sunlight on her elbow and on the rounded nakedness of her shoulder, the downy glow. He felt unusually elated at the thought that he would see that naked elbow glowing in the midday sun more than once that day. He hadn't realized yet that he'd fallen instantly, irrevocably, and hopelessly in love.

And then, as if by miracle, the crowd parted and he saw all of her at once: the face gleaming with freckles, the ginger curls brushing the expanse of bare shoulders, the sharp line of the slitted skirt along the skin of her thigh, the breasts almost naked under the sheer tank top, and the way she brought her hands together as though about to applaud. Or was she sending him a covert message, unnoticed by her entourage?

Her eyes lingered on Alec's face. She had caught his stealthy glance, and now she knew that he knew that she knew that he was watching her. It was easy enough to read in his eyes (rigidly unblinking from strain as he tried to pretend they were occupied elsewhere) the same message that was written in the eyes of dozens around him: Here was a monster desperately in need of love. He buried himself even deeper in the newspaper, hoping to conceal the bags under his eyes, the dog's collar of fat under his chin, his cheap Soviet-style spectacles with the twisted metal ear pieces. Alec even turned his head a little to make less glaringly obvious the receding hairline. But he might have suspected that in those bags under the eyes and that double chin and that receding hairline (not to mention the twisted necktie dangling from the shirt collar with the top button missing), this young Russian recognized something familiar and homely. He wouldn't be surprised if his appearance triggered some instinctive gut feeling from her half-forgotten childhood—the family dinners and birthday gatherings with relatives: the loud, meaningless babble, the squeals of joy and the endless kisses, the fat bellies, bald patches and flabby chins, the sagging bulldog cheeks and broken spectacles. She carried on with her idle chatter, accompanied by the approving and chortle of her accidental acquaintances, among which she now included that bald head with the clumps of hair protruding from behind the newspaper.

Meanwhile Alec inched his way along the bar toward her, still pretending to be interested in nothing but his newspaper. He struggled stubbornly to take in the story skipping about the page before his eyes, one of those typical *Daily Telegraph* courtroom reports about a middle-aged woman who, together with her lover (a flying instructor, by the way, who taught her to fly not just in bed), had decided to do away with her spouse, a bigwig in the Ministry of Transport. The most absurd thing about the story was the lethal means the killers had adopted: a lawn mower. A gigantic lawn mower, like a tractor. And a lake had played some part in the proceedings as well. The lovers had intended to give the husband a tap on the head, and then seat him on the lawn mower, and then drown him. Alec couldn't get his mind round the absurd combination of flying instructor, lawn mower, adulteress, and transport minister. But he hadn't really been reading; he'd been listening. The clear tones of her voice cut through the buzz and cacophony of idle prattle, the chink-chink of glasses.

She was talking about some aristocratic English lady's travels in Russia, a Lady Beecham or Chatham (Alec didn't quite catch the name from his corner of the bar), who during her train journey through Russia was accidentally left behind with a lapdog on an empty platform on the Trans-Siberian railway. The whole point of the story, as far as Alec could tell, was that an entire train was sent from Vladivostok on Lenin's personal orders to save this English lady and her Pomeranian, and that upon arrival in Moscow, this lady set off directly to talk with Lenin in the Kremlin. "Just imagine an English lady with a Pomeranian dressed in nothing but a dressing gown with Lenin in the Kremlin!" Most of her exposition was devoted to the mystical nature of Russian geography and other tortuous complexities. All this time Alec kept his eyes glued to the *Telegraph's* account of sexual escapades and the lawn-mower murderer illustrated with photographs of the principals.

Listening to the Russian voice from the other side of the bar, Alec was mesmerized by the absurdity of it and the incongruity of her own presence here in the pub, with her bizarre stories of a British aristocrat and the Bolsheviks. In fact, it was every bit as absurd and inappropriate as his own presence here, in this pub, on this street, in this city. It was simply that he wasn't living in his own time. Like every émigré, Alec lived in a different time—the time of his emigration. His age in this new territory was measured in time served as an émigré. He was discovering things that only kids were supposed to be enthusiastic about. He was constantly drawn to the younger generation—

and also, as it happens, to young girls, such as this garrulous, freckle-faced girl who could have been his daughter.

At the moment his mind registered the fact that he could no longer hear the Russian cadences of her voice prattling away. He looked around in panic; he couldn't believe she'd disappeared, just casually finished off her kir and not said goodbye to him—if not in words, then at least with a nod of the head, a lift of the eyebrow. Hadn't she let him know with her gaze that she knew he was watching her? And hadn't he let her know that he knew that she knew? Alec began elbowing his way through the hubbub and the crush of the pub, stepping on feet, proffering excuses to right and left. Someone swore at his back, "Bloody Irish!" but he didn't attempt to clarify his ethnic origins. He popped out onto the street like a cork from a bottle of champagne (that favorite tipple of Soho revelers).

She was nowhere in sight. There was still heaps of time left till evening, but Soho was reeling like the deck of a tourist skiff overloaded with drunken, yelling passengers. The entire city seemed to be celebrating. But the reason for the celebration remained a mystery to Alec. Nobody had informed him about this party, and he hadn't been invited to join in.

Then suddenly she surfaced right under his nose. Or rather, she appeared at his shoulder, as though from the next room, from a little door hidden behind blinds between a sandwich shop and a place that sold uniforms for valets, doormen, waiters, and the like. Clearly not noticing that Alec was standing a centimeter away from her, she screwed up her eyes toward the far side of the street, looking for something she apparently hadn't been able to find on her side. Alec was standing close enough to see drops of sweat beading her freckled temple. As she cut across Frith Street, she halted on the boundary between sun and shade to pull up the slipping shoulder strap of her tank top, and then a sharp twist of her hip carried her entire body forward and her leg emerged, bare almost up to her knickers. Alec licked his dry lips. She had a purposeful look about her. At the next block she stopped in front of one of those windows that stand out among the colorful clutter of the Soho streets precisely because they lack the slightest trace of showcase allure, so that an uninformed individual might easily conclude that the shop is closed for repairs. Or else that it isn't a shop, but a rental office, a warehouse, a bookmaker's, or a returned tickets office.

Alec watched how purposefully she strode into the establishment. He crossed the street and went up to the window. The glass was rendered totally opaque by the bills pasted to it— for a striptease show, a double act, a peep show, video booths, and something mysterious called "poppers." The place was called Supermag. He could feel himself beginning to blush to the roots of his hair. A sex shop. Porn. Before parting the bamboo blinds to enter this monkeyhouse, Alec looked around furtively. And immediately he had the entire picture. His beautiful stranger had appeared from another establishment of the same ilk across the street, with a pink neon sign advertising unisex, serial, and every other possible kind of love—through a peephole, on video, with cloven hoof, and in triune combinations of all type, size, and race. So the establishment into which she had just disappeared was not the first of its kind. Taking a deep breath and suppressing a feeling of disgust, tremulous curiosity, and sick fear, Alec cautiously pushed aside the bamboo blinds. They clattered in a way that was far from sexy, the way the wooden beads on an abacus might.

Inside, the monotonously stupid disco beat usual for such places was absent; it was quiet and decorous, with a vague smell of dust and books—very much like a public library, with shelves of magazines and videos. A provincial museum of ethnography might look like this, if its native masks and shaman's instruments were replaced by pink rubber vaginas, inflatable sex dolls, and vibrating dildos, and the walls were hung with sadomasochistic paraphernalia, from leather corsets to tassel-tipped whips.

To conceal his confusion, Alec plucked a magazine of some sort out of a pile and stuck his head in it, executing the same ostrich maneuver that had served him so well minutes before in The French House. From the corner of his eye he watched his quarry loiter for a moment by the shelves of videos, then set off purposefully and without the slightest embarrassment toward the hulk at the cash register. He lumbered out from behind the counter, looking very menacing.

Mysterious explanations and conversations commenced, with Alec's beautiful stranger making those passes with her hands that he already knew so well. "Nothing but American: not French, not German, but American," she insisted, as though everything was perfectly normal, the only unusual thing being that inimitable Russian lilt in her melodious voice. "Nothing else," Alec heard her repeating, as though speaking to a foreigner, loudly and with exaggerated emphasis. With an air of baffled indifference, the salesman pulled aside a blind to reveal a low shelf of videos, and she bent down to examine the cassettes one after another. Alec gazed at her bare back where the tank top had ridden up from the skirt stretched tight over her backside.

Alec sighed abruptly and swallowed hard. He didn't know what to do with himself. His hands still clutched the open magazine. His eyes eventually came to rest on a vagina, which gazed out at him like a gigantic swollen eye. He barely had time to close the magazine before the face of the hulk with the mustache from the cash register appeared.

"Soft porn, hard core, or maybe gay? Or perhaps you'd like a rubber doll, sir?" The bruiser leaned over him politely, gesturing round the shelves like an Italian ice cream salesman. Meanwhile his ward cast a blank farewell gaze round the premises and strode off decisively toward the exit. Alec elbowed the salesman aside and dashed after her.

The same thing was repeated in another sex shop, then another one. Everywhere the same procedure: She entered the shop with the determination of a clerk entering a bank, cast a quick, experienced glance over the contents of the shelves and turned to the shop assistant, always with the same question: Where could she find an American video? In one place the round red stickers on the various boxes meant the tape inside was American; in another porn shop, the American cassettes were labeled with the mysterious word "hobo." Every time, Alec squeezed himself into the most remote corner of the store. There was nothing for him to do but grab hold of the nearest porn magazine while straining to hear her dialogue with the shop assistant. When he'd exhausted every move and every excuse for loitering in the shop without attracting her attention, he waited for his ward on the other side of the street like a cheap private detective, pretending to read a newspaper or looking casually in the shop windows.

He was gradually drawing his own conclusions. Her peregrinations among the sleazy establishments of Soho only proved what the tabloid press had been saying for some time now: London was teeming with girls from Russia. The export of young girls was now a thriving business. It was hard for a Russian to resist that kind of money. She'd probably been told that some of her clients would be American businessmen, lonely in London, looking for sex. That was why she went round looking for American videos in sex shops. Or perhaps she was doing it on her own initiative: Russians are crazy about America.

After a while, Alec felt a terrible weariness come on: another sex shop, then another shop—there were too many and he was alone and he couldn't possibly keep up with her. He slammed the magazine shut; it was time to put an end to this voyeurism. He was morally and emotionally bankrupt—not to mention the pitiful state of his finances. There were too many holes in his heart and in his pockets.

"Soft porn, hard porn, gay videos, sir?" The manager approached him, offering the standard bill of fare. In the darkness it seemed to Alec that he was wearing a Jewish skullcap.

"Yes, I have a question on the subject of videos," Alec said, surprising himself with the brazen insolence to which despair had driven him. He put it nakedly: Just what exactly was the essential and precise difference between American porno flicks and others? His companion shifted his skullcap to one side and scratched his head.

"I think it's all a matter of plot, sir," he replied thoughtfully, gazing at Alec as though to assess his intellectual capacity. Alec gawked at him like a nanny goat reading a poster or a billy goat watching a striptease. "The Americans like to develop the plot, you see," the wise man in the skullcap explained. "First this way, then that way, and then the other way. Right? But the Germans get straight into it, without bothering about with story lines: this way, that way and the other way, all at once! Do you see what I mean?"

"Well, sort of. . . What about the others? The French, for instance?"

"Well, you know what the French are like, sir. What the French want is something a bit out of the ordinary, a bit of something off the beaten track. First this way, then that way, and then the other way. Right? *Comprenez?*"

"No, I don't *comprenez* at all," said Alec, starting to get annoyed. "Sex is sex. When it comes down to it, everybody does the same thing, no?"

"The same thing, sir?" the manager asked with a frown of concern. "Surely you're not telling me you don't know the difference between plot and narrative?"

"I need examples. It's too abstract," Alec mumbled, almost apologetically. "I don't see it, as Stanislavsky used to say."

"I understand." The man in the skullcap nodded solemnly. "Stanislavsky. I see. Are you from Russia, then? If your intentions are serious, I'll show you some examples, sir."

When Alec had confirmed the seriousness of his intentions, the instructor selected a handful of cassettes, and led him to a dim corner where a video screen was hung at eye level, garishly lit by a wall lamp in the crimson-purple tones of a bruise. Yawning, he inserted a cassette with indifferent, almost somnambulistic, dexterity.

"French," he announced lackadaisically, folding his arms

and closing his eyes to take a little nap. A few minutes later he inserted another cassette: "German." And retreated into unconsciousness until it was time for the last: "American." People who trade in vice are rarely themselves addicted to vice, just as a cobbler never wears his own boots—they're just too expensive.

"Okay," Alec said as the film continued to run on. "French, German, and American. But why is the same blond in all of them?"

The porn instructor shrugged. "Nowadays all the stars are international. National boundaries are being erased, sir. It's the New World Order."

In the reddish darkroom gloom, the pasty white face of the shop manager floated like a lurid moon beneath its strange headgear, which Alec now saw wasn't a Jewish skullcap at all, but a sort of truncated nightcap, with a tassel hanging down one side. Even in this light he could see that his mentor's face was furrowed with pockmarks.

And now in a moment of blinding epiphany, Alex recognized him: He was a street bagpiper. In the evenings he could be found on the noisy corners along Shaftesbury Avenue from Piccadilly to Tottenham Road, outside the open doors of the pubs and cafes. Sometimes he was let into the expensive restaurants to drum up business when they opened in the evening. On such occasions he would change into his kilt with a sporran and short jacket with a white lacy shirt, and on his head he wore that very same cap with the dangling tassel. And now in hindsight Alec realized that the hulking brute with the false mustache in one of the other shops was the spitting double of the waiter in a Turkish restaurant he'd been to. The other character, the one with the sharp features and tweed cap, was obviously the traffic controller from the nearby minicab office. Soho's porn industry was populated with people who appeared in different roles depending on the time of day. Some people knew them as waiters, traffic controllers and bagpipers; but at other times they turned up behind the counter of a sex shop. That was it precisely: parallel worlds beyond good and evil.

From a corner of his eye, almost with the back of his head, he suddenly sensed the presence of a third witness in the lurid semidarkness: Her lips tightly compressed, she was gazing in rapt, unblinking fascination at the American-style porn video. Perhaps it was the crimson reflection of the lamp that made Alec think that even in the semidarkness he could see her cheeks flush red in shame. But something made him sure that she had seen him, perhaps the slant of her eye—or was it those little daggers of irony at the corners of her mouth?

"What do you think you're doing, spying on me?" she called out in a clear, ringing voice. His neck and shoulders tensed as though to receive a blow, but he couldn't bring himself to stop, because he didn't know how to answer her. He forced his way through a crowd of revelers and idlers, past the cafes and bars, as though in one of those dreams when you run even though you know it's impossible to escape. She was already running, almost level with him, yelling into his face: "Do you think I haven't noticed you following me around all day?"

Alec was on the point of giving her the answer she deserved, but just at that moment his heel slipped on the asphalt and his ankle twisted under him, so that he lost his balance and went tumbling backward and to the side, straight into the arms of his beautiful scandal monger; if she hadn't grabbed him from behind, he would have cracked his head on the pavement. A cherrystone skidded out from under his heel.

"I almost broke my neck because of you," said Alec, taking the offensive. "That's *your* cherrystone."

"That cherrystone? Mine? Has it got my name written on it or something?"

"I saw you buying cherries. And then spitting out the stones. Not nice. What did they teach you at school?"

"That's just what I was saying—you've been spying on me!" his blue-eyed dish announced triumphantly, clearly proud of being able to prove her point. But he paid not the slightest attention to her riposte. He was drinking in the tiniest details of her face, seeing them now as if from a distance of a centimeter through some gigantic telescope. Everything was so magnificent, so symbolic, so beautiful: the bead of sweat on her upper lip, the down on her temples, her freckles, the flare of her nostrils, the wild blue of her eyes—if he once dived in, he'd never surface again. Suddenly he'd forgotten all about his bald patch, his double chin, his pot belly, and his frumpy old spectacles. His hands felt heavy and his heart felt light.

"Maybe I was just doing my usual route?" The long-absent note of irony was back in his voice.

"It's not your route. You were following *my* route." Her brows slammed indignantly together above the bridge of her nose.

"Everything in this world is relative," he intoned solemnly. "Our routes just coincided." After all, she'd gone into the last sex shop because he was there. Who, then, had been following whom? That was the question. "Was I following you because you were following me or the other way round?" And he launched into an elegant argument to the effect that if routes coincide, how can you tell the hunter from the quarry?

"Why on earth would I want to follow you?" she exploded. "I'm not the slightest bit interested in you."

He turned away with exaggerated indifference, as though to leave, but she instinctively moved to block his escape, putting out a hand that almost reached his elbow; now she had to prove she was right. He stopped and turned back to her. "With all this preoccupation about being followed, I think you've been watching too many movies," he sneered, finally finding his stride. "*American* movies, to be precise." He saw her lips tremble, her fingers clench into fists and then unclench again, as though warming up to deliver a slap across the face.

"This just proves my point. You've been eavesdropping on my conversations in all those shops, haven't you?" At last she'd turned up incontrovertible evidence of his quasi-criminal intent.

"I wasn't eavesdropping. I just happened to hear you, that's all. I could hear a voice like that with my fingers in my ears." And he pantomimed sticking his fingers in his ears to shut out a persistent noise. She blinked at him, astounded at such effrontery. Yet again he'd caught her off guard and wriggled free of her clutches. She threw up her arms in a gesture of despair and incomprehension, like a schoolgirl who's failed some idiotic exam.

"Go to hell," she spat. "Spying's a filthy Russian habit. Watching how other people live their lives. It's no better than a cheap porn show."

"How do you know I'm Russian?" Alec asked with a frown. "Is it written on my forehead or something?"

"How?" she retorted. "That accent of yours. Or is it

African then?"

"It would appear we have the honor of belonging to the same national minority."

"What makes you think that? I haven't got any accent."

"I was eavesdropping in the pub," he chuckled. "About the English lady, the train, and the Pomeranian. 'Maybe the dog could have grown along the way?'" She laughed despite herself at the sound of the line from the old familiar childhood text. The street stood still for a moment, entranced by this laugh. Alec took her by the arm and, switching into Russian, said "Let's go. People are looking at us."

"Right, let's go," she agreed immediately, pronouncing the Russian consonants with a strange English softness, laughter still lingering on her lips. And she added, "I've been dead on my feet all day. I want to sit down somewhere."

That was what he'd been waiting for her to say. With girls like this, a restaurant was an essential part of the procedure. He fingered the last fiver lying limply in his pocket. More than one of his checks had bounced that month, and his only hope was the old hole-in-the-wall. Due to the chaos in its computer system, the bank continued to give him money from its cash machine, but according to his own calculations, he'd already extracted his weekly norm from that source too. Apart from anything else, however, he hadn't seen any bank machines along the route they'd followed, and he was afraid to turn off the familiar trail: She might turn off onto a trail of her own, and it would no longer be his. Then he had an incredible stroke of luck: On the corner of Shaftesbury Avenue he came across a Westminster Bank cash machine that didn't spit out his card; instead, five crisp ten-pound notes slid out into his waiting hand. For the second time that day he smiled in happiness.

Passersby were gaping at them in idle curiosity because he was standing there beside her—an incredible contrast, positively spellbinding—or perhaps she was simply so well known here in Soho that everyone recognized her face. Damn the lot of them, anyway; let them envy the old codger his luck.

People on the sidewalk seemed to make way for them, but Alec used the crush as an excuse to brush against her shoulder, her hip, her bare elbow. Stepping out beside her, he stole a glance at that damp lock of hair swaying at her temple. Unlike him (who was soaked with sweat from the tension), she seemed to relax completely once she'd told him exactly what she thought of him, and she strode along with the carefree air of an absentminded tourist, peering idly this way and that. When they found themselves back at the bar of The French House (they'd both instinctively followed the familiar route), she was instantly engulfed in her usual entourage of admirers-cum-entrepreneurs—or perhaps sugar daddies or plain, ordinary ponces. Or were they all perhaps her clients?

"What's so charming about this place," Lena went on, "is that everyone pretends to know each other, but in actual fact nobody knows anything about anyone—or even wants to." Alec tried to interrupt to interpolate a witty observation of his own, but she stole the words right out of his mouth: "Here you can adopt absolutely any past you like."

"So who do you like to be taken for?" Alec asked.

"I don't like to be taken at all. I just sell myself. Visually," she said, looking him straight in the eye and sipping her kir. She was standing by the window, and at that very moment the clouds drew slightly apart so that the sun lit up her profile like a newly cleaned section of an old oil painting. Once again, a ray of light caught the delicate ochre down on her elbow, and Alec reached out to run a finger across it.

"What *is* that?" he asked with an almost childlike astonishment. "Why can I only see it in the sunlight?"

"Because it's dyed," she said, jerking her arm away. "Haven't you ever seen dyed hair before?" And then, abruptly changing the subject: "Will you be in London long?"

"How do you mean?" Alec asked, rather taken aback. "I *live* here."

"So you're an émigré?"

"I'm not an émigré. I'm a subject of Her Majesty," he added with poorly concealed pride, referring to his British citizenship.

"And is that all you do?" Lena inquired archly, taking another sip of kir. "You look like a teacher."

His feathers ruffled, Alec replied with dignity: "While you—how did you put it?—sell yourself visually. My vocation is in sound."

"I see. That explains why you followed me round the sex shops: to eavesdrop, not to watch."

"I'm not an eavesdropper, I'm a broadcaster." But then he immediately began lying again. "As it happens, I'm doing a program about sex shops for the BBC Russian Service. There's a lot of interest in that now in Russia. Being bilingual, you'd be ideal for a job at the BBC," he added hastily. An instinctive tactic: Once it becomes clear that you can't repel the alien invader and will have to coexist with her, your best bet is become her patron and mentor. Begin by making her a protégée, an assistant in your ventures and dreams, and eventually she'll end up a slave of your émigré empire. He felt like a character out of

Kuprin or Bunin: a White Russian with a fallen woman in a fallen city, or something of the kind. They would broadcast together during the day, and in the evenings sit by the fire and listen to their own voices on the air.

"My father's in broadcasting too, Voice of America. He's in Washington," Lena explained. But she was in London—a typical example of the new species of economic migrants. He imagined the carefree father in his comfortable America, not suspecting how his daughter earned her living or where she spent her nights. A sense of indignation at other people's dereliction always restored his own self-confidence. His temporary embarrassment vanished without trace, and with the facile volubility of a playboy and man of the world, he began instructing her in the dangerous twists and turns of London life.

I see him there, no longer squeezed into a corner by the crowd: The force of his eloquence and confidence have established something like a protective barrier around him. It's clear that he's a man who has trodden the boards, and now the ranks of the public have fallen back before him (even though this performance is not being played out for them, but exclusively for Lena). His voice grew strong, his eyes glowed, and he was no longer merely speaking, he was pronouncing *ex cathedra*. He was ready to help her. He could introduce her to his circle, show her London's most remarkable places, and she wouldn't feel so much like a homeless stranger, condemned to wander the streets of Soho alone.

"Will you be in London long?" he asked politely.

"How do you mean?" She was rather taken aback. "I *live* here." And she explained that she'd been brought to London via Israel at the age of seven by her parents, who were "third-wave" émigrés. A familiar story. No doubt her parents were from the same generation as Alec. He could even have come across them standing in the queues for visas. He almost choked on his whiskey and water thinking about it. An urgent change of conversational direction was required. It seemed she was the one who should be lecturing him about life in England, not the other way round.

"But anyway, have you been practicing this—what did you call it?—'visual selling' of yourself for long?"

"Ever since I finished college," Lena said with a shrug. "I experiment with photographs. That's basically my profession."

"The oldest in the world," said Alec with a wry smile.

"But it's badly paid," said Lena.

"That obviously depends on the client," said Alec with a sympathetic nod.

"If it wasn't for my Americans, I don't know how I could have survived this year on nothing but unemployment benefits."

"Americans always pay well. During the war they paid with cigarettes and bully beef."

"They still pay well, but I prefer cash. It's a huge corporation. My father set me up with them."

"What kind of corporation's that? I don't understand. You mean to say your father pushed you into this business?" Alec was totally flabbergasted. A father putting his own daughter on the game. This was some kind of murky Dostoyevskian perversity.

"My father has connections in advertising. The Americans have this crazy thing about statistics. They want to know what percentage of pornographic videos on the British market comes from America." Since Alec had invited it, Lena didn't hesitate to plunge into shop talk. It was amazing, wasn't it, how generally illiterate and unrealistic people were. How could there be any statistics, after all, when no one had a clue how to tell an American video from a British one, not to mention French and German? Especially since all the cassettes were pirated copies, copied over and over twenty times or more, and virtually nobody had ever even seen an original.

Alec was gradually (and, in a way, even reluctantly) compelled to see that Lena had elbowed her way out of the niche he'd settled her in, and was talking not about prostitution but about a demographic study she was doing for some firm of American pollsters. They were paying Lena to find out how American pornography was doing on this side of the Atlantic, and without bothering to concoct any grand strategic scheme, she'd set off to rummage through the shelves of Soho's sex shops.

How very unimaginative his own dirty thoughts had been. Alec blushed.

"The porn clerks just don't want to hear about it," Lena continued indignantly, paying no attention to Alec's discomfiture. "And why should they? Just look at them! One's an assistant manager on the night shift at McDonalds, another's the minicab traffic controller from that place on the corner, and another's a part-time Scottish bagpiper, for God's sake. Did you notice that?"

"I certainly did," said Alec, finally recovering his voice. So he would suggest the following tactic: Lena and he would have to pretend to be a couple of foolish tourists from Russia. After all, hadn't they taken each other for new arrivals from the old country? Alec, with his Russian accent, would talk to the sales-men in each sex shop about his Moscow friends' taste in videos. He could say everyone in Moscow was interested in American porno films. Because America and Russia were twin brothers. Anyone could be made to believe that. After that they could ask any questions they liked—what percentage, what made them different, how many did people buy, in every sex shop—just as though they were following a questionnaire.

"Alec, you're a pure Guinness," Lena said in her remarkable Russian. But what Alec registered was the intimate way she used his first name.

Everything in Soho was the same as it had been an hour earlier, but for Alec it was an entirely different street, with dif-ferent faces and even different weather. Amazing how such a thing can undergo total transformation as a result of a few ten-der words whispered in your ear—not even whispered, but simply imagined in the gap between a couple of smiles, a single ambiguous glance, and the jingling of change in your pocket against the background roar of a crowded bar. With every glass of kir, it must be admitted, the clinking of change in Alec's pocket became fainter and fainter, and soon it was being drowned by the clattering of bamboo blinds and bead curtains at the entrances to sex shops: But the clattering was no longer like the rattle of beads on a bookkeeper's abacus. Now it was an invocation on native drums and tambourines.

Lena and Alec no longer lurked or sidled as they entered these establishments, no longer glanced around furtively. They strode in together arm-in-arm, as though visiting a wax museum or a fairground hall of mirrors, bubbling over with laughter in anticipation of yet another idiotic stage turn. Alec himself was transformed beyond all recognition. Even the gleam of his bald pate seemed to have acquired a sense of purpose; as though a headwind had deliberately whipped away his hair so that it wouldn't hinder him as he pressed onward to his goal. The spectacles with the bent frames that had seemed so oppressively ugly now presented themselves as the elegant functional appurtenance of a true professional. The unbuttoned shirt collar above the tie, even the pot belly hanging over his belt, had suddenly become visible signs of the hardened journalist's contempt for external presentability; all that was lacking was a cigar in his mouth and a notebook with a massive fountain pen. He breezed into sex shops like a sanitary inspector into Soviet food stores—someone to be expected, braced for.

In each establishment Alec got down to business and explained that for some reason Russians preferred American porn. Affecting a tourist's naiveté, he inquired what it was exactly that lent American videos their special charm. Were they only popular with Russians, or did the English like them too? And so on and so forth. Lena was absolutely delighted, and he had the ecstatic feeling that the entire world was one big sex shop, and they were the ponces working in it. Along the way Alec also managed to tell her the story of half his life. By the time they found themselves in an establishment bearing the name "Double Act," Alec had completely abandoned all caution and restraint, together with all his complexes about his English and his Russian accent, as well as his ridiculous émigré appearance.

The green door, daubed with graffiti and pasted over with a random medley of posters, had an ominous air of such unapproachable gloom that he hadn't immediately noticed the sex shop sign above it. The two of them, Alec and Lena, took turns to tug at the door handle like mischievous children—there was no bell or knocker. Alec, grown impudent at this stage, was readying himself for a kick at the door, but just at that moment the door opened of its own accord. They stepped into the black chasm of the entrance and found themselves in a typical porn establishment anteroom. The walls were covered in a black funereal crepe material illuminated by dull red lightbulbs. In the crimson glow, the face of the hulk who emerged from the black crepe looked like some genie out of a bottle; his muscles rippled up toward the ceiling like tautly inflated balloons, and every move he made was accompanied by a jangling of chains and spurs. The door was on such a powerful spring that even this genie had to use both hands to hold it back. The guardian raised his chin in a gesture of inquiry. Alec immediately launched into his usual spiel about Russia, and how he was a tourist and he'd promised his friends in Moscow to bring them some videos, but they all wanted American porn, and nobody knew how to choose the American videos, Gorby-Raissa, polar bears, Sputniks, Hindi-Russky. He was beginning to regret that they'd ever stepped inside this particular den of thieves.

"Boss!" the punk genie growled over his shoulder in the direction of the bamboo and bead curtains behind his back. "We've got some Russians here."

"Unarmed?" a powerful rumbling bass inquired out of the darkness. "Tourists. A diplomatic mission. Shall we arrange a reception committee?"

"Let them in," the bass rumbled. The Hindi or Muslim

guardian parted the bamboo curtains behind him with a powerful hand, passing Alec and Lena through to the interior.

As though ground to dust in a pulverizer, the rosy light of a setting sun filtered through a bubble-textured window in an infinite number of bright droplets. Sitting in this fine shower of sunlight, as though bathing his face in it, was the master of ceremonies of this elaborate stage setting for lust.

The first thing to catch their attention were his bare feet in house slippers made of tartan felt, darned and comfortable in their ordinary ugliness. His large, balding forehead was covered by the plastic peak of a baseball cap. But most impressive of all, his only clothing consisted of a spacious tunic or toga over which he had donned a vest of the sort favored by soldiers and terrorists, with an infinite number of pockets for bullets, grenades, and bombs of different sizes. But newspaper cuttings rather than bombs protruded from the pockets. Newspapers lay in a heap on the small table beside him, and torn-out pages littered the floor. In that tunic, with his unshaven chin and that heap of newspapers, he seemed like a man who has only just risen from bed to take his morning coffee. There was in fact a coffee pot on a tray beside him. Even as Alec and Lena stood there like supplicants before the throne, he was leafing through the newspapers, perusing them from top to bottom with professional precision.

"Our kind Italian neighbors bring us this," he said at last, peering up at them through his spectacles and taking a lazy sip of coffee from a tiny cup on an equally tiny saucer. "Our English brethren have chosen to prefer the magic herb of China and India over the West-Indian coffee bean of America. But why are the lady and the gentleman standing? The lady and gentleman are not in some public city square. Chairs for the lady and the gentleman!" He waved his hand, and the punk-Sikh-Hindu-or-whatever guardian pounded off to fetch two chairs that it might once have been possible to call Venetian.

Alec recognized that voice; it was the voice of the town crier, a voice that seemed to cancel out the mask of the pensioner in slippers reviewing the evening paper. Alec encountered him every now and then outside the famous restaurants of the West End where he was invited to amuse their tourist clients, and he wasn't dressed in a tunic and domestic slippers there, but in white stockings up to his knees and shoes with bows, in full livery and a wig, with a bell tinkling in his hand. He would ring the bell and then, with a resounding, rumbling "R," would start up his "O yea, O yea" and follow up, just like the BBC radio, with the main news of the day.

It was not difficult to see that this role at the porn shop suited him better than yelling at the top of his lungs in the rain and fog about natural catastrophes and murders and acting as though nobody but him ever read the newspapers. Now it was clear why he had such a pile of them: He was apparently preparing for his evening shift, gathering material for his stentorian declamations. Alec picked up on the town crier's comment about Chinese tea and American coffee and began a brief exposition of the purpose of his visit to the sex shop, that ended with a question: What made American porno flicks different from all others, especially British?

"The answer's very simple: in every way, and not at all," the street crier replied, knitting his brows. "As Shaw once observed, Britain and America are two nations divided only by a common language. We English have a different sexual language. A different *oral sex,* so to speak. We prefer *talking about sex* to sex itself. Preferably over the phone. Sound plays an immense role in the development of a national pornography. What would a porn film be without sound? Nothing!"

"I know," Alec nodded in energetic agreement. And then, with a poorly concealed note of snobbery, he blurted out, "No need to tell *me* about the significance of sound. I work for the BBC."

Lena stamped discreetly on his foot, and Alec barely suppressed a yelp.

"The BBC?" the street crier hissed through his teeth, contemptuously raising his bushy Brezhnev eyebrows. The punk bottle-genie whistled in extreme disapproval and rattled a bunch of dildos together threateningly, the way housewives clatter dishes in the presence of unwelcome guests. "So you're not from Russia at all," murmured the town crier with a menacing scowl. Alec squirmed and began trying to put things right, rattling on about how he was *from* Russia, only just not from the *present* Russia, but rather from a Russia of the recent past—the very recent past—but nowadays there was extensive cooperation between Russian radio and BBC radio, which meant he was on an internship with the BBC, for an exchange of broadcasting experience, you see, so that while he might not be from Russia just at that very moment, he certainly was from the Russian airwaves. While he was reeling off all this nonsense, the town crier puffed away on his cigar and leafed through his newspapers, licking his finger and not looking up. When he came across something of interest, he immediately nipped the article with a deft movement and dispatched it into one of his little pockets. Alec couldn't spot how the town crier managed to cut out the articles so precisely, as though wielding an invisible pair of scissors.

"To take a single instance," Alec forged on desperately, "on the topic of Russo-British links in broadcasting, we thought it would be interesting to find out just what the specific features of British sex are. And what parallels there might be with Russian, so to speak, erotic culture." Alec stammered to a halt again.

The herald continued to leaf through his newspapers. Then he looked up at Alec. "I see you read the press organ of the British conservatives, the venerable *Daily Telegraph*. There was a certain little article in it—" He reached out toward Alec's pocket and unceremoniously plucked out the newspaper that had been resident there all afternoon, opening it at the relevant page. "About how the headmistress of a grammar school and her lover, a flying instructor—have you read it?—tried to get rid of her husband." He made a single deft movement, without asking Alec's permission, and the article fell out of the page in an astoundingly regular rectangle, as though cut with scissors. But it wasn't scissors. Alec had finally caught sight of the instrument involved—it was the town crier's own elongated thumbnail, an immense nail sharpened to a knife's edge. Goose pimples raced up and down his spine.

"It would appear, my dear sir and madam, that the lovers' nefarious plan was simple but original: Give the husband a light tap on the head, seat him on a lawn mower, set it moving in the direction of a pond, and the husband would drown—an accident. Elementary, my dear Watson, don't you agree?"

"You call that elementary?" Lena laughed.

Out of the corner of his eye Alec watched as the mustachioed Mexican—the same one from "Supermag"—emerged from the blinds at the back to have a whispered conversation with the punk-Indian. A moment later the two of them were joined by yet another member of the porn coven: the pock-marked bagpiper.

"I have given you no more than a mere thumbnail sketch of the intrigue," said the town crier, continuing to finger the newspaper cutting. The bright idea was as follows: When the husband mounted his wife the headmistress, the flying instructor would creep up from behind and hit him on the back of the head, just stunning him slightly; then they would seat the husband on the lawn mower and point it directly at the pond. (As though the husband had had a heart attack, and he'd had no time to step on the brake.) However, there was a small hitch: The idea of copulation with his own wife was so unusual to the husband that he became terribly aroused, and as soon as he'd run down to the summer house, he stripped himself naked. That didn't suit the conspirators: After all, what English gentleman would ever dream of trimming the lawn in the nude? And so his wife began insisting that they must start their love games with their clothes on. She must have told him that the more complicated the process of undressing, the more aroused she would become or some such lie. This was what differentiated British sex from any other sex in the world, the complexity of the process, said the herald.

"Is that not a similarity between the English and Russian nations? In Russia, ladies and gentlemen walk around in the skins of wild animals, do they not? It might seem that the process of unfastening hooks and laces would destroy the charm of erotic coupling. But not so! This did not render the act of copulation in wild animal skins any less attractive than it is we must assume for naked savages on an African beach."

"So the most powerful orgasm would take place on the North Pole?" Lena asked ironically.

They were interrupted by the meowing of a fluffy white cat that looked like an immigrant from Siberia. It peered out from between two stacks of videos and then leaped from there onto the powerful black-skinned shoulder of the Indian-punk-genie and from there onto the heap of newspapers in front of the town crier, where it settled and began chewing on a news clipping.

"It makes the material easier to remember," said the town crier, as though it were not he, but somehow the cat who digested the news to play the declaiming fool on the fashionable squares of London. He scratched the chomping cat behind the ear like Goldfinger in the James Bond film. All these circus tricks—the cat chewing on news articles, the fantastic stories about sex with lawn mowers: They were simply pulling the wool over their eyes, keeping them occupied while they decided how to get rid of the pesky Russians journalists without leaving any traces. It seemed to Alec that the criminal rabble in the corner was tightening the ring. It was time to cut and run.

"By the way, what actually happened to the Minister of Transport on the lawn mower?" Alec tried to sound casually sociable as he retreated in the direction of the exit. The cat was chewing up the last fragments of the love story as they watched.

"Oh, the husband came round, disentangled himself from the lawn mower, and swam to the opposite bank," said the town crier. "The flying instructor was unable to follow, because he couldn't swim—he only knew how to fly. Where are you two going?"

"It's time for us to be making a move too," said Alec, without it being clear what he was referring to, and he took Lena by the elbow.

"After taking nourishment our cat also requires a turn in the fresh air," said the town crier, grabbing the cat by the scruff of the neck and tossing it up into the air. The cat landed on the shoulder of the bagpiper, now arrayed in his full Scottish finery. He grimaced in disgust but took the cat into his arms. A collar glinted beneath the cat's chin. Forcing themselves to smile and bowing as they went, Alec and Lena backed toward the exit.

"Where *are* you going?" the town crier asked, waving his arms in their direction. "We were so looking forward to hearing about sex with Russian bears."

Alec hurried out of the room. The Mexican with the mustache was standing in front of the bamboo blinds like he had a pair of revolvers hanging from his belt. The bagpiper with the cat got up and started to follow them. "I have to take *my* wildcat out too," Alec tossed the words back over his shoulder as he and Lena dashed out into the street.

London is a city that respects privacy and it is also in the habit of separating trading premises from residential areas. It is a dark city; this makes the brightly lighted areas of ill repute, like Soho, seem even brighter than they really are. Alec and Lena skipped out of the antechamber of the sex shop into the street as though they had stepped out from the dim wings of a theater onto a stage flooded with light. Evening time Soho greeted them with a cocktail of drunken roars, the egg yolk yellow of gaslights, the hissing of neon and culinary fumes from kitchen ventilators.

But as soon as they turned a corner it became clear that they really were being followed: The bagpiper was moving through the crowd on the other side of the street. That white cat could be seen from a mile away. What kind of nonsense was this? Nothing else could have been expected. That monster with the baseball cap and razor-sharp thumbnail, that pseudo-traffic controller of minicabs with the Mexican-dagger mustache, that genie-punk-ponce—the entire porn mafia had clearly decided to combine forces in order to terrorize this pair of spies masquerading as Russian tourists. They had to get as far away as possible from this den of iniquity on Piccadilly, and Alec glanced back over his shoulder as he threaded his way through side streets leading across Shaftesbury Avenue toward Leicester Square.

In this state of what seemed to him to be mortal danger, Alec recovered anew a sense of the wholeness and the meaning of his winding path through life; once again he felt decisive, daring, agile, and bold, surrounded by enemies and the frost of Russia. Alec felt hot the same way he had felt hot in the bitterly cold frost of Moscow, where his eyes were seared by the blinding snow instead of blazing neon signs, and his shoulder ached from the weight of a heavy suitcase crammed full of manuscripts. He had plowed his way through the snowdrifts of Brezhnev's Russia toward the Dutch embassy in order to send his samizdat out to the West, and the entire street had seemed to be watching his back; at any moment a plainclothes agent might grab him by the collar. The suitcase had eventually been successfully delivered to the West. But when he read his Moscow manuscripts in London the words lost all meaning as though the Moscow he'd known had never existed. That Moscow life had continued to exist, but without him, which of course meant it could manage without him, which in turn meant that his presence there in the past had been without meaning. We would like our love to die together with our betrayal of that love. But love can exist on its own—without any country or suitcase, with no bottom to it and no lid.

And now as he fled from the sinister bagpiper through the London crowd, he squeezed his fingers tight round Lena's hand in that same trembling presentiment of disaster that had tightened his fingers round the suitcase handle that time in Moscow. Lena seemed to have sprung out of the hole left in his life by that suitcase. Every step on the trail he had followed that day now acquired purpose and meaning. He was terrified and deliriously happy. He was where he belonged. He was home, surrounded by enemies, saving his friends. What in the world could be more nostalgic? What doesn't change from one country to another? Classical music? The scent of fresh-mown grass? Of course. But also the feeling of danger. The sense of threat. Pain. The right of citizenship is acquired through fear.

Frightened to death by the criminal denizens of Soho, Alec was no longer an outsider on this street, in this world. Taking Lena by the arm, with the clarity of vision of a brilliant strategist, he mapped out a route that would confuse their pursuer. He knew, for instance, that there was a mirror in the window of the shop that sold uniforms on the corner of Old Compton Street, and they could follow their enemy's movements while appearing to be looking in this window, the way spies did it in films. Their pursuer, meanwhile, made no attempt to conceal either his purpose or his presence. The crowd parted before him as he was pulled along by the cat straining on its chain, just like a dog: The angora albino was on their trail, sniffing out their scent in the pubs, doorways, and shops.

"Hey there, stop, hey!" yelled the Scotsman in the kilt, trying to attract their attention. Or so it seemed to Lena. But Alec was convinced that the gestures were signs to his accomplices from the porn underground and found a way to give them the slip at every turn—a back alley, a back doorway. Lena was amazed that he knew all these byways and passages. Presently, he and Lena had discovered that they both lived on the south bank of the Thames, where there was no Underground, only mainline trains; they would have to make their way together across Leicester Square to Charing Cross Station, avoiding their tail, and in this commonality of route Alec discerned yet another hint at a *vita nuova*. There was no more Russia, no more England. No more East and no more West. There was only the two of them. He felt he'd known Lena almost since she was a child; it was just that they hadn't seen each other for ages. The exotic foursome (three without the cat) swung out on to Charing Cross.

There they began fighting their way through the crowd, which, like the faithful of some obscure sect, had silently massed before the electronic signboard to read its fate in the train timetable (half the trains having been canceled and the other half terribly delayed). Alec's trained eye instantly spotted the platform they needed, and the train was due to leave in seconds. From the corner of his eye, he saw there was no way the bagpiper or his cat could possibly break free of the crush in time to overtake them. They galloped toward the train, but at the very last moment the heavy iron gates at the platform entrance rumbled and slammed shut before their very noses, like the Iron Curtain in the face of a Soviet émigré. The conductors' whistles sounded, and the carriages rattled and rumbled away.

They turned back to find the bagpiper looming up in front of them, the cat twining its leash around his bare legs in their gaiters.

"Like the story with Lady Beecham and the Pomeranian, isn't it?" said Lena. They were being crushed against the iron gates by dozens of others who had missed the train—all bound with the same chain. With a cat on a dog's leash.

"Hey, hey, Russki-Russki mensch," the Scottish bagpiper said to them in what he probably took to be a soothing mixture of Russian and Yiddish, moving closer.

"Shove away!" Lena shouted, trying to ward him off with an émigré solecism. But Alec, wasting no time on solecisms, grabbed her by the elbow and made a dash for the side exit, down the steps to Villiers Street, down there, under the vaults of the station cellars and the arches of the railway bridge where the drunks and deadbeats gathered, half-asleep and half-drunk.

"Change, change!" they whined, their hands outstretched for petty alms at every corner. But the word *change* can mean more than just the small coins in your pocket; it can mean a turning point in your life as well, and Alec, worn witless from all the running, swore to himself: "What kind of change could possibly happen in this country?" Then he suddenly realized that the passage they'd turned into was a dead end. Ahead of them was a wall of hands outstretched to demand either the pennies in his pocket or fundamental reforms in his way of life. There was no retreat. As he heard the bagpiper's footsteps closing in on them, Alec found a narrow niche in the wall and squeezed himself and Lena into it.

The next moment the bagpiper with the cat on the leash appeared at their niche. Alec didn't believe in nonviolent resistance. He squeezed himself tightly into the gap in the wall and clenched his teeth as he waited for the circumcised cap with the tassel on the head of the bagpiper to draw level with him. It was the tassel the cat jumped for, breaking free from its chain when Alec sent it flying with a blow to the back of the neck. He flung himself on the bagpiper with all the dexterity of an experienced gangster. Then, giving the bagpiper no time to recover, he kicked him square in the balls. The bagpiper squealed, doubled over, and collapsed onto the asphalt, squeaking at every one of Alec's blows like his bagpipes. Alec felt he was acting in defense of the weaker sex (Lena) and national minorities (émigrés) and supporting the struggle for freedom of speech (in sex shops). Alec turned away from the bagpiper and the cat when, tracing an arc through the air, the furry Siberian jumped straight atop Alec's bald patch. He in turn squealed and sprang back in fright, waving his arms absurdly. The cat fluffed up its tail and meowed as it leaped down to the asphalt, and slipping through the legs of the crowd of idle onlookers, darted off in evasive zigzags under the arch and into the street. Alec slumped against the wall in exhaustion. He was breathing asthmatically.

"Fucking psycho!" the bagpiper swore, turning to Lena, his face contorted in fury. "Will you kindly explain to this bloody Russian of yours that I have a fucking business proposition for him? Business, understand? Us here, you there—in Moscow, okay? Videos, okay? Moscow-London, London-Moscow, sex shops, joint venture, okay?"

Recovering his breath, he began again, explaining that no one had wanted to scare them: The bagpiper himself had been scared half to death. He wanted to offer them a deal—without his town crier boss in the sex shop knowing about it. He'd been wanting to cut a secret deal. The export of American and any other videos to Russia. And from Russia to England—girls. In short, their own porn business. Lena would make an excellent barmaid or even a madam in a brothel. They could set things up on a big scale, with branches in Chicago, Glasgow, and other countries.

"And at the same time we could teach Russian to anyone who was interested," Alec suggested tentatively as he pondered the possibilities of this unexpected idea for a joint venture.

In passing, the bagpiper confessed that he wasn't really a Scot at all. He came from a family of Ukrainian émigrés, but he was proud of having grown up in Scotland and he regarded Robbie Burns as the Scottish Taras Shevchenko. What did Alec think of the idea of a Ukrainian-British porn film about Taras Shevchenko and Bloody Mary? With Puss-in-Boots?

"Wait!" he said, looking around in panic. "Where's the cat?" He began running around in circles, glanced round the corner, into the niche, running halfway to the street and back. He was pale and trembling. "I've lost the cat. The boss'll sack me," he kept repeating, wiping the blood from his lips and the sweat from his brow.

The point was that the bagpiper had set off after Alec and Lena without his boss knowing anything about it, simply pretending to be taking the cat for a walk. The town crier was fonder of that cat than of his own mother; they might even be living together as a married couple, and if the cat disappeared the bagpiper would pay for it with his head—quite possibly in the literal sense, because the boss had connections with more than just crazy lawn mowers and genies out of bottles. If he couldn't find the cat, Soho would be off-limits to the bagpiper once and for all, and he had no life outside Soho. And they could kiss goodbye to all their dreams of a Russian-British joint porn venture.

They began combing the streets block by block. But the cat must have been the one with the original seven-league boots hiding somewhere over the rainbow or up the beanstalk. In the end Alec was so moved by the bagpiper's mental anguish that he declared himself willing to have a personal word with the boss about the cat's disappearance. Once free of fear, Alec began to remember (or at least imagine) that he was an individual with a certain standing and connections in the world. He was prepared to make amends for the loss of the cat by offering the town crier a chance to collaborate with the BBC Russian Service.

However, no such extreme measures were necessary. As always happens in London, everything turned out well in the end of its own accord. When they reached the Double Act sex shop, they could hardly believe their eyes: The fluffy white beast was squatting there on the doorstep, assiduously licking its coat, washing away the dirt of the past and evidently preparing for sleep. Several newspaper cuttings rustled on the pavement in front of it. The streets of Soho were emptying, its clubs sucking in the last few revelers like the final drops of marrow from a well-gnawed bone.

"Cats always find their own way home," said Lena, "only by very complicated routes."

"That sounds like the English formula for sex," said Alec.

"Where all the charm is in overcoming difficulties along the way, just like the Russian formula for sex," said Lena, reminding him of the lessons of the day gone by as they rode home in a taxi.

They really had turned out to be neighbors. As he walked Lena to her door, he wondered what parallels he could find in his relations with Lena if they were to become lovers: Eric Gill, who slept with his daughter, or Stanley Spencer, who was supposed to have had a liaison with his younger sister? Or was that Byron who had a thing for his sister? Alec wasn't Byron, that much was certain. But he was an exile like Byron, and of course Lermontov before him. Letting Alec in after only a brief moment of hesitation, Lena remarked cynically, "I picked up my first client in Soho after all."

"That was the idea," Alec replied, but even he didn't expect the trail to be so long and winding.

THE NOTIFICATION

1. A LETTER FROM MOSCOW

His wife wasn't coming. She couldn't come just now. Or she'd never intended to come. It had been so long since he'd received her last letter from Moscow. There was no longer any point in blaming the post office or the sinister censorship offices in his mind's eye. As usual, he dozed off almost immediately that night but soon woke up and, tired of tossing and turning, got out of bed to write another letter to the black hole of his wife's mailbox. This latest letter of God knows how many, sounded like some Chinese ultimatum, repeating the same idea over and over again of settling scores and figuring out who left whom. It was pointless. She still wasn't coming.

He finally fell asleep at dawn, just in time for the daily morning dream. It was disturbingly real. Once again he is walking down a hallway in his Moscow apartment block. Once again he turns toward the huge array of rectangular, light blue mailboxes in the wall and notices something white in their box. The box is locked, but there's a long slit the thickness of a finger and several pinkie-sized holes, and if he bends over he can see that it's a postcard. He reaches for the key to the letterbox, but all the keys are left in the apartment. And he can't get into the apartment. His wife has the only spare key. He tries coaxing the postcard through the narrow slot. He gets a finger on it, and now carefully works it out to where his other hand can grab it. The card slips. It is so close. It falls back to the bottom of the box. He glances in through the holes, tries again. This time he sticks a finger through one of the holes and tries to push the card up toward the slot. He reaches the ragged line of stamps, just barely manages to turn the card round, and now has to get his hand a bit higher, supporting the card from below so he can carefully push it up with the one finger, but it bends and threatens to wriggle free. And now he's at it with both pinkies, but the card slips free and falls to the bottom of the box again. He's exhausted. He takes his hand out. His fingers are bloody, the skin torn, and he can't get the handkerchief out of his pocket because he doesn't want to get blood all over himself.

"Cleaning! Cleaning!" The shout saved him. The cleaning lady was in the corridor, her insistent knocking combined with that shouting brought back the old fear of strict orders, the need to escape, the hasty leave-taking, and the fear of flight into the unknown. That single foreign word had become so familiar that it had lost its strangeness. It sounded just like Russian, and once again, he was confused, not sure where he was. Regulations in the Israeli hostel for immigrants were strict.

Jerusalem was of course just a layover on Mark's journey to the West from his native Soviet Russia. An undesirable and antisocial element in the eyes of the Soviet authorities, he secured an exit visa without the slightest difficulty and was forever barred from returning to the Soviet Union. His departure had been quick and painless except for the fact that he left his wife behind.

Mark let the cleaning lady in, grabbed the insomniac letter, and set off downstairs. The words he had written were still echoing in his head. He felt guilty. He was the one who had linked his life to hers and then confronted her with the impossible dilemma—choosing between their marriage and the sum total of her life in Russia: friends, family, all of it. When he glanced with feigned indifference at the hostel's pigeonholes for mail, there was a letter. He grabbed it greedily. It was from Moscow, marked "express delivery," registered and plastered with cosmonauts and many a Lenin. He suppressed the trembling of his hands and stopped himself from opening the envelope straightaway. He fingered it slowly, guessing at the thickness of the letter. He wanted to find a comfortable bar in town, sit down with a drink, and savor every word, gradually, with relish. Then he would decide whether or not to send the letter he had written the night before.

It was cold—it had snowed the day before—and although the sky had cleared there was a chill in the wind. This time when he touched the envelope he felt a wave of hot air. His Moscow past and his Jerusalem present collided with an emotional bang. And then it was a chilly January day once again, like the day he arrived. He shivered in the cold wind. He wanted some hot soup. Hot bean soup.

Mark walked past small factories. The pounding of the hammers and the flash of the arc welders greeted him. This was Mammila Street. He liked the name. It reminded him of "mama." There was a diner here that made good bean soup with fantastic marrowbone. He was in a part of town where faces were swarthier, either because they were born that way or became darker from welding and tinkering with metal. He wouldn't meet anyone who knew him here. No one would ask if he'd moved out of the hostel to start his new life with a loan for a fridge and a mortgage for an apartment. Mammila Street led to the gates of the old city; it was a real street with rows of tall buildings—so rare in this ancient town and strangely reminiscent of Moscow. The diner was simple, cozy, and clean, old-fashioned in its own way, with marble tables. Its owner was a stocky man with a friendly dark face, always polite and helpful, never rushing his customers who were mostly truck drivers and local workmen.

It was still a bit early for lunch. The diner was empty. He sat at a table in the corner, facing the street, and looked at the cold sunlight streaming across the tables and the counter. The owner remembered Mark. He yelled to the boy in the kitchen: "Bean soup, good and thick!" As he brought pita bread and beer to the table, he told Mark that the marrowbone was unbelievably rich and tasty today. Mark ate slowly, picking out the soft pulpy beans with his spoon. The soup was piping hot and spicy. He washed it down with beer. He then wiped his plate clean with some pita, the way regular customers do, pushed it away, lit a cigarette and sipped beer, glancing out now and then at the street. Only then, with the ambience of the diner, the hot soup, the beer, and the sunshine did he feel sufficiently settled. The beer had cleared his head. He was ready to open the envelope.

The haunting dream of the night before began to fade away in backlit swirls of cigarette smoke that moved toward each other from opposite sides of the diner, met in the middle, and scattered in a haze of golden motes. The air was drifting, and the whole room began to sway in time with it. Mark wasn't surprised when he noticed a crumpled figure opposite him in a dim, sunless corner. He was sitting at a table with his head resting on folded hands, and to judge from the shaggy gray hair, he was an old man, but Mark couldn't be sure, because it was obvious at a glance that the hands lying on the table were strong and young. There was an empty glass in front of him, and a small puddle of cognac on the table glowing yellow in a splash of sunlight that had just found his cheerless corner. The sight of a man sleeping like an old drunk was unusual for a place like this. Mark forgot all about him as he took the letter out of the envelope and began reading:

I spent a long time wondering whether or not I should write to you, or whether I should wait to see what your next letter was like, but then, damn it, I decided to rise above this epistolary kitchen brawl and send you a card. After a visit to the post office I had to go to a birthday party—you know whose. Since it was very early I went for a walk I really enjoyed walking: it was warm, not too damp, and when I left the market stalls by the metro I was on an absolutely empty boulevard, and it was a bit frightening, even though it was still light outside. I wasn't in any hurry. It was like I was observing myself from the outside—you know the mood that comes over you sometimes, as if you're watching a film about yourself: there I was sending the letter, here I am walking sadly through a wet, deserted square and remembering all the previous birthdays when I walked through this square just like this one but not like this. It's really quite an optimistic mood to be in, because in a film everything's so simple: after these frames come the words, "Twenty years passed," and you know that in the film there will be something in twenty years' time to wait for. . . . But all the possible versions of my life in twenty years' time are not worth filming, too dull and sad.

He stopped reading. The letter was a month old. His reply would arrive after another month had passed and she wouldn't think it was a reply to this letter, but to the one she would write when she got his last letter, and never the twain would meet. Dappled sunlight slipped across the large, childish handwriting, and then suddenly, the way everything happens in Jerusalem, the sun sank behind the tall buildings and immediately it was twilight in the diner. The lingering light from the sun and the fluorescent light created the strange feeling of events adrift in time, as though the slightest move might change the direction of everything. Mark coughed as the smoke caught with his breath.

Afterward I went home half drunk, and as I staggered toward the door of our house, I realized that I have nothing to hope for, except the miracle that some day when I come home you will be waiting for me and I won't have to fumble through my bag with drunken fingers to find the key, I'll simply ring the bell, and you'll open the door. How could you? It's murder, nothing but murder. How could you do it? As I sit here crying I am convinced that it can't be true, it can't be true that you are gone, it's all a bad dream and in a moment I wake up. Of course, this awaking from a nightmare is only a wonderful dream, but in reality it won't be so romantic, you'll probably just turn up in this country some day after years and years, and you'll find a nasty, old, weary, irritable woman without a husband.

Or else you'll finally turn up here and find an irritable old man without a wife, Mark thought. He squinted blankly. The man in the corner raised his head in slow motion and looked at Mark. When their eyes met, the man lowered his eyes, raised the empty glass to his lips, and tipped it back, watching for a long time as the last drop of cognac slithered down the glass without reaching his lips. He looked up at Mark again. This was no ordinary old man; it was an emaciated ruin of a man. With this the man stumbled to his feet and came toward Mark's table. Mark instinctively covered the letter with his hand. Without asking permission, the stranger sat opposite Mark who looked away as he stuffed the letter back into the envelope.

"Do you write letters?" the stranger asked in Russian. It was startling to hear Russian at this diner where Mark came at least in part to avoid the vulgarity of provincial Russian that was all too common in Jerusalem. "Do you write letters to your wife telling her to come right away, bickering about who left who?"

"What do you know about my wife? And how's it all the sudden your business, anyway?" Mark growled.

"First, there's a ring on your finger, and there's a woman's name in the return address," the man went on in his slippery Moscow patois. "You see, I'm an expert when it comes to letter writing. You don't know what words mean to a woman. She will never forgive you for being put in a position where she was forced to admit that she was wrong. I realized that words can kill a long time ago. I used to write letters to my wife too. My hands are the same as they used to be. . . ."

He raised his hands and spread his fingers, and Mark saw with distaste that his hands were young and strong—stained with ink and scratched, but young and strong—as if they were borrowed from some other body. He rubbed his hand across his face in a sleepy gesture and leaned toward Mark again.

"When time comes to part, it's easy for people to trick themselves into thinking that the ones they left behind somehow betrayed them. We all breathe the same air, and it's not that difficult to convince someone that for every breath they take, someone on the other side of the planet is choking to death. You'd do better writing letters to the solar system; it's just as much to blame for everything. Especially in this place," he said, glancing over his shoulder at the banging of the door as though he were expecting someone. But it was only the strong draft of the winter wind. "You don't know Jerusalem; the people here cannot be their age. So many peoples and civilizations have rolled through this place before you got here, everything that's going to happen to you has already happened to someone who was here before you. You can't find a new life here. You can't find a new death. You can't find anything new. And make sure you stay away from old women offering comfort, too. You won't like what happens. You'll become a museum exhibit. But before any of this happens, may I ask you to buy me a drink?"

Mark's face was distorted by a combination of irritation and boredom, but the young old man took no notice of this. A shot of brandy clearly revived him.

"Shall I tell you how I die? I mean to say, how I'll die in a few hours?"

Mark was silent.

"Tell me, how long does it take for a letter to get from Jerusalem to Moscow? If we assume it's not censored, because why censor a notification of death?"

2. CONFESSIONS OF
A LETTER WRITER

I've always felt an unhealthy curiosity about other people's lives and an almost contemptuous indifference for my own. Other people's lives always seemed to form a complete whole. I can only guess that it was precisely my shapeless, chaotic character that constantly drove me to try on other people's lives as if they were clothes I might need to wear sometime in the future. Each time I was disillusioned. But the desire to break away from my own private chaos drove me to take another's life again and again—not kill them, you see—but follow it carefully, listening and watching and imitating. Perhaps it was this constant desire to change my own fate, to trap it, this desire to escape from my skin. I think that's why I left Russia. It may also be the real reason I feel attracted to older women who know just how, when, where, and what they want. In their hands you realize who you are, and who you could have been but never will be. Almost all boys have dreams about a woman like that. I met mine right here where we're sitting. As though all my life I'd just been waiting for just that encounter.

In fact I'd been leading the idle life of a professional nobody of the sort that can only exist in Moscow. I found work with old people, or somehow got connected with them. I worked as a reader for blind professors. I liked reading out loud to someone who couldn't see me, as though I were dictating my own thoughts and feelings. I worked as a nurse for lonely old women, and when I heard them all tell me the same stories, I began imagining myself in their places. And of course I was always scribbling something, a kind of diary. A friend actually suggested that I write some reminiscences about an actress who died during my watch. Not actually write them, of course, but take them down from her husband, a doctor who had loved her madly and had supported her all her life. He also looked after her. For more than half her life she had been severely mentally ill. I think it was my friend who knew that he was looking for someone to write an article about her based on his own memoirs and other archive materials. It wasn't so much writing the article that attracted me as the way the two of them had lived together.

I began visiting him. He was a tall old man, still strong, driven almost out of his mind by his wife's death. But he still worked as the head of a local clinic despite his age, and even though he had plenty to retire on. You know the sort. He was a man of the old school who stubbornly refused to understand the changes going on around him. The irreality of his work was obviously his defense against the reality of her death. He had truly adored his wife, treating her like a spoiled beautiful child. She really was an extravagant woman: seductive looks, provocative behavior. Most of the time she was away from home, touring the provinces with her theater company. But her earnings were unreliable, she was often ill, and all day long he had to dash from one hospital to another, from one patient to the next, while she had little affairs with great men right under his very nose.

Perhaps her husband guessed at what was going on, but judging from his character he probably thought a great actress had a perfect right to behave that way. Having said this, he wasn't completely simpleminded, because he didn't show me the most important letters. I used to visit him in the afternoon when he came back from the clinic, and with meticulous attention to detail he would lay out plates of food prepared the day before and uncork a bottle of Georgian wine. He always laid the table generously, filled up my wine glass, and then invited me to the table with a gesture that made it impossible to refuse. He would sit beside me and watch while I ate, as if he were fattening me up for the slaughterhouse. He'd keep on filling up my plate until the food and the wine made me feel sleepy, and then he'd say: "Shall we do a bit of work?"

He had a huge apartment in an old Moscow house. It had the unavoidable air of death and neglect about it. All the rooms were stuffed with heaps of old newspapers from the far corners of Russia with reviews of his wife's tours. The yellowed, dusty bundles were piled up so high that they even blocked the windows. On the way to the table you had to maneuver between the newspapers and files and photograph albums. The plates pushed aside, we would sit at opposite sides of the table. I would have a bunch of newspapers and he would have the glue and scissors and his homemade album turned to a new page. The photographs and reviews were arranged in chronological order. He wrote out every review in longhand, even when he had dozens of copies.

"When she was unwell," he would say for the hundredth time, tears welling up for the hundredth time, "and I had to go out to work, she stayed at home, the poor woman, and when I came back she would be tearing the reviews out of the album, the ones that criticized her wonderful acting, and you know she was wonderful, quite, quite wonderful!" At night—I'm convinced—he would lock himself in his room and take out the prize letters from her, the ones he stubbornly refused to show me, and copy them out by hand. And not for the first time, either. I'll bet that when he'd copied the entire bundle, he'd start over again, saying he hadn't done it nicely enough. He wrote in a large old man's scrawl that was almost impossible to read. Maybe those unreadable copies the old man wrote out were the key to the whole business. From the beginning to the end, they were essential for the article I was writing, but he wouldn't let me see them. He just sat across from me, watching to make sure I didn't miss a line from the monotonously rapturous local reviews. After a while, the same reviews began coming up a second time, but still he kept on dragging things out, refusing to let me read the letters.

Sometimes he would pass me a review he had read, with the critic's brightest compliments marked in red pencil, and make me read them aloud. At some stage she had obviously given up on French vaudeville, and took up with different army theater groups as well as a trade union theater. Then there was the mysterious incident, a kind of bad joke, when she was summoned by the KGB and questioned, and she refused to answer. I'm not sure what was it about, or when it happened, but once when I decided to ask him what really happened, he chewed on his lips for a while and then said: "When my poor darling became really ill, she began going around with her arms up in the air all the time, and when they asked her what she was doing, she said she was upholding the party line." He didn't smile as he told me this, not even wryly; he was so politically naive that he didn't see the terrible mockery in it. But he could sense what I was reading on the pages of a newspaper, because when my eyes slipped idly across to some other curious story, he always noticed and asked me again to pay attention to the "inimitable talent" out of some review I'd already read a long time before.

Sometimes as we were drinking tea, he would look me in the eyes and ask: "How's the article coming along?" But at a certain point I realized that I was the only person on earth he still talked to, and he wanted to keep me with him as long as possible. Meanwhile I'd developed an authentic fear of the undiminishing mountain of newsprint in the apartment. The widower still kept on writing out the letters that he cried over. The turning point in our relations came when I saw a photograph of his wife in one of the albums, a photograph I hadn't seen before, and was struck by the uncanny resemblance to a woman I knew very well.

The old photograph, glued to sturdy, pre-Revolutionary cardboard, showed the actress at about forty years old, with her usual expression of affected wantonness. She was posed like a ballet dancer, with the train of her dress wrapped around her and one foot pointed at the small of her back. I stole it and brought it home to compare it to a snapshot I knew only too well. It showed a woman lying on a couch with her head resting on her elbow and smiling a strange smile: That is, it wasn't the smile that was strange, it was the combination of the eyes and the smile—the eyes had been crying and that turned the smile into a grimace. It was a snapshot of my wife. She often had this expression at the later stages of our married life. The resemblance between the two was uncanny.

It all started with that mysterious similarity. I began feeling differently about my wife. A thought crept into my mind: Perhaps my wife was a bit of an eccentric too. She took the nightmarish life of Soviet Moscow far too lightly. She felt no fear of the KGB at all; she didn't jump at an unexpected knock at the door. I could no longer bear going to see the widower with his newspapers and letters. I'd started to think I was turning into him, and my wife was turning into the mad actress walking around with her hands up in the air to keep up the party line. I began to see the entire country as this widower's room, where some old guy sits opposite you and makes sure you read the same newspaper article over and over again, full of sickly sweet compliments to someone who has nothing to do with you and all the while making sure that you don't see any of the good stuff. When I tried to explain all this to my wife, her face went blank and closed, and she said that there was no way we were leaving Russia.

It all came to an end when the two of us were invited to a dinner to mark the anniversary of the actress's death. The table nearly cracked under the weight of all the food they'd laid out, the widower was flanked by two or three solemnly silent relatives with tight neckties and sinewy wives, but almost all the places were taken up by the widower's colleagues from the clinic and hospitals where he'd worked: sly, plump women doctors and raucous ward sisters. They knocked back the vodka and stuffed down the food. One of them put some fish on my plate while the widower was giving a speech—interrupted now and again by a senile cough to hide his tears—about his "unforgettable wife, immortal spirit and incomparably gifted laborer of the arts." My neighbor leaned her shoulder against me and babbled into my ear: "Eat up now, critic, you little sausage, eat the trout while you have the chance." It was nothing like trout, some other kind of smelly river fish with tons of bones that I choked drunkenly on while trying to put on an attentive and cheerful expression.

I noticed that the widower was addressing his memorial

speech to my wife, sobbing as he leaned over toward her, and she was already the worse for drink and was stretching out her hand toward him. I suddenly remembered the similarity between the two photos. I stood up, knocking over my chair, staggered around the table to grab my wife's hand, and moved for the door. The host hurriedly bent his senile head to kiss my wife's hand, and said to me: "Till tomorrow then. Shall we carry on with our work?" The next day I didn't go. And a week later I applied to leave the country.

I shouldn't bother explaining to you that emigration from Soviet Russia to the West at that time was like an escape from Nazi Germany—there was no chance you'd be returning to see your relatives, friends, lovers. We spent months arguing about my wife's decision not to join me. She thought that I'd simply decided to leave her. Then she was saying that I was incapable of considering what she wanted once I had decided something for myself, and surely I didn't have any problem stepping over her dead body. Then she said that she couldn't go just now, that with her bad heart she couldn't move to a climate like that. The climate was just another excuse. The year before she had a different reason, and in a year's time she would have another one.

I was granted permission unbelievably quickly, everything happened with quite mysterious speed. That shocked my wife even more. Until the very last day she acted like she was packing my things for a business trip. I had no friends left, and the apartment was filled with a resounding silence. She walked back and forth between the suitcase and the closet, sometimes asking questions as she checked the list of my things. When she asked whether I'd remembered to buy a toothbrush, because the old one was absolutely worn out, I was so astonished by the almost insane banality of the question that I opened my mouth to shout at her, but I saw the coldness in her eyes and kept silent.

The night finally came when we were left entirely alone, my last night in Russia. She was lying on her back with her eyes closed. I was lying next to her, and I closed my eyes in an attempt to get to sleep, because the plane was at five in the morning, so I had be at the airport by four at the latest, and I'd have to wake up even earlier. I tried to focus my thoughts on waking up, and not think about the fact that my head would never touch that pillow again. Then I felt my wife turn over on her side, and through half-open eyes I saw she was lying with her face pressed into the pillow. I heard her begin to cry. Then the crying became a quiet wailing, a suppressed sobbing that made my ears ring even though it was barely audible. And for the first time in our sad life together I knew there was nothing I could say to comfort her. I couldn't offer comfort anymore, and I couldn't cry. I had no strength to change her mind or per-suade her to come with me. All the words had already been said. "Stop crying," I said, and turned to face the wall. "I won't," she said, like a disobedient child, and sobbed as she thrust her face back into the pillow. "I'm going to cry until I die," she muttered, "to make you understand, so you'll know that you've killed me." But in fact she was afraid of being with me in a strange country, knowing that she wouldn't be let back into this one, afraid even that this fear of hers was a failure of trust and a betrayal of me, and it was she who was leaving me—but I doubt she could admit that to herself at the time or even later on for that matter.

"You couldn't care less if I die here reading piles of news-papers about a crazy dead actress while her old husband keeps an eye on me. You look so much like her, why don't you just

move in with the old man? The two of you would make a perfect couple; he can mourn her, and you can mourn me." Since
that conversation we had essentially stopped talking to each
other. Until that final night.

While she lay there and wailed with her face in the pillow, all
those mutual reproaches of unfaithfulness kept going round
and round in my head, fusing into a single irritating buzz
around my temples, forcing out the last drop of regret and at
the same time bringing about the strangest kind of anger, like
the kind I'd imagine people feel right before they commit suicide. "Do you want me to return the visa?" I asked her, almost
certain what the answer would be. She turned to face me, raising her head from the pillow, and I saw her red bleary eyes,
drained of their last tear. Her face was distorted.

"Only madmen and sadists abandon their wives. I hate
you," she said in a half-whisper, "I hope you die there, I hope
you're alone there, but may you first go out of your mind from
loneliness, become a ruined old man without a friend in the
world, and then die and then rot." And she dropped her face
back into the pillow. The rotting part was like an afterthought.
A nice touch. I lay there without moving, staring up at the ceiling. The ceiling began to look like a low gray sky ready to
unleash a torrent at any moment. I turned away in a panic and
lay there looking at the wall, aware of every breath I took and
every one she took, and soon I wasn't sure whether I was really
lying there and staring at the wall or I was dreaming that I was
lying and staring at the wall. Then the alarm clock went off, but
in my half-dream I had already heard myself hearing the alarm
clock go off so many times that when it did go off, I wasn't sure
whether I was dreaming it or it really had gone off. Outside the
window it was still as dark as ever, but you could tell that it

would soon be dawn. I raised my head to look at the alarm clock and it was time to get up. My wife was either asleep or pretending she didn't hear anything.

I took a long time to get washed, trying to wash away the sleepless night and everything that had been said. Then I surveyed my swollen features, sagging like an old man's face, and the bags under my eyes, and I thought that was how I would look in thirty years. Then I went into the kitchen and switched on the light. You know how disgusting it is when you switch on the light on a winter's morning, when it's pitch-black outside, and you know that you have to start living, to wake up and leave. I spent a long time grinding the coffee in the electric grinder, secretly hoping that the loud buzzing would wake my wife and things could be cleared up. Then I began brewing coffee in the old jezvah—the little brass thing with the broken handle—and when I took it off the gas, wrapped in a towel, I still managed to burn my finger, and I cried out exaggeratedly, but she went on pretending that she didn't hear anything. Then I began drinking the coffee, glancing round at all the petty details of a domestic life I would never see again. I looked at the slipper stuffed under the door so that it wouldn't bang in the wind. The old, useless wooden coffee mill. At the crack just below the ceiling. At the set of ladles and spoons, a house-warming present that we'd never used, left hanging over the stove. I carried on acting as though nothing had happened, as though I had simply woken up too early and was going on a business trip, and I looked at the black sky, which was just beginning to turn gray, like the bedroom ceiling a little while before. The television tower was just taking shape against the sky, like a shadow at night on the ceiling. Then I looked at my watch and stood up. I put on my winter coat, checked that my gloves were in the pockets, and picked up my suitcase. It was no good. Not that way, not without even saying good-bye, I thought, and I put down the suitcase. I went quietly back into the bedroom and switched on the light even though it was already quite bright—the room lit with that unpleasant effect when artificial light isn't needed, casting a dull metallic glint.

She was lying there with her face stuck so deep into the pillow that only the top of her head could be seen above the blanket. I sat down in my coat on the edge of the bed and quietly spoke her name. I could make out the shape of her shoulders under the blanket, her back and her hips—they were probably warm from sleep—and she looked so familiar there in our bed, and outside it was a shudderingly cold winter morning.

"Won't you at least say good-bye to me?" I asked uncertainly, and put my hand on the blanket. "Well?" I called her name again and gently shook her shoulder. Then I bent down and kissed her, that is, I didn't really kiss her, I just pressed my lips against her neck behind her ear, brushing aside a lock of her hair. I was surprised by how cold her skin was, or rather not the coldness, but that she hadn't grown warm in her sleep. I shook her again, but still she didn't stir. I shuddered. I began shaking her violently, angry in my surprise, and I flipped her over onto her back. Her body was heavy. Her head slumped back on the pillow, and the motionless, tear-stained eyes stared at me. I threw back the blanket and tore open her nightshirt and bent down and pressed my ear against her.

I still didn't believe it. I took her hand at the wrist and felt for her pulse for a long time, but I wasn't sure that was the right place to look for a pulse, and if it wasn't, where else should I look? I went into the bathroom, glanced at my own pale face and then washed it again. Then I went back into the room. I remembered what I could do: I held the small mirror to her closed, motionless lips, trying not to breathe. It didn't mist over. Nothing stirred. This time, I fearfully touched her face with my palm; I jerked my hand away: Her face was damp and cold. When did it happen? During the night? She hadn't even cried out. Or perhaps she did cry out, and in my dream I heard the alarm clock ringing again. Or nothing happened in my dream. I had slept while she died. I had slept with a dead woman in the bed and not felt a thing.

I went toward the telephone, but then I stopped and hesitated. I'd actually wanted it to happen. She said she would cry until she died, and I'd wanted it to happen, and I hadn't said a word. If I hadn't actually wanted her to die, I'd wanted her to disappear. So that I could finally be alone. This brought the finality I'd secretly been working for. And that feeling of calm indifference. There was no need to phone anyone. They would manage just fine without me. Just as they had before. I imagined in fright what would happen if I picked up the phone: the autopsy, the relatives loitering in the apartment, the funeral and the wrangling with the crematorium, the long lines at the offices, the documents, and then more documents and more relatives, the drunken wake, and I would never get away. Then there would be the anniversaries. I remembered the old man with the drunken eyes and the cough making his memorial speech. I never had fulfilled my promise to write about his wife. I grabbed the handle of my suitcase, after fastening all my coat buttons, and went out, slamming the door behind me. I had already pressed the elevator button when I changed my mind again and went back to the door. I opened it with my key. For the last time I opened it with my key, then I put the key on the floor in front of the door and left it open. The elevator wasn't working, and I set off slowly down the stairs. Outside, the morning air was frosty and damp.

Jerusalem greeted me with a cold, transparent, bright-blue sky, as though that was the way the sky had always been. The light in Jerusalem had an immediate effect on me. Have you noticed that here it's either very bright—piercingly bright—or pitch dark? As bright as bones in an X ray, as though you could see people's skeletons through their skin. But when it gets dark, it's so dark you might think the town doesn't exist at all; there's just the wind roaming over the hills. Perhaps it's because they cover all the windows with blinds and you can't see a single light in any house where you might find friends waiting for you.

Maybe you shouldn't listen to me. I stopped listening to people almost as soon as I got here. Of course, at first I felt liberated. I didn't know a word of the local language, and at first I felt as though I was caught up in the torrent of a strange and colorful life with great prospects ahead. Then the color faded, and it turned out that the only people I had to talk to were people I half-knew from Moscow, fellow émigrés. Nothing had changed. But they had definitely changed. They had changed in the sense that every one of them was trying to prove that he had changed, and trying to use that change to substantiate the decision to move.

They had moved here in the hope of becoming new people, but the question of whether this hope had any substance was a taboo subject. In secret (even from themselves) they all belonged to that club of people who live by the conviction that the place they have come to is the best place on earth. Not because there aren't better places, but precisely because they came here. They weren't prepared to admit that we're members of a lost generation that was born with the desire to emigrate. Once a man has thought about leaving a place, he's already pretty much slipped through the net. Of course no one wants to think of themselves as an émigré or an alien. Thus the Russians stubbornly tried to pretend that they were related to each other, even as they suspected each other lacked family feeling and so kept trying to find out if their relatives really felt they were among family or not, and if they didn't then they had to be watched with a colder eye and made to feel their waywardness.

I didn't understand this at first, and I went on treating each of them as I had back in Moscow. For some time, I kept on meeting old acquaintances until it became clear that I wasn't dealing with the person I'd known before, it wasn't him answering me, but the mask that he'd pulled over his face. I haven't been here much longer than you, but I've had time to see people's faces grow that new layer of skin, so that only the glint in their eyes stays the same. And then later on even the eyes grow new skin and the person you used to know is gone. I stopped going to see my friends when I figured this out. In one of the last conversations I can remember, someone said:

"People should be born where they intend to die." And some-one quipped: "Does that mean you should live where you are already dead?"

One night, huddled up under my government-issue blanket in the hostel and struggling to find the secret door that leads to sleep and forgetfulness, I remembered my wife. I turned onto my back and there again was the ceiling, looking like a gray sky. And stretching across the entire sky in the darkness outside the window was a white, arching scar, like frozen lightning. I sat up in bed, and the scar shifted across the black vault. Unable to understand what was going on, I rolled over, but the scar in the sky followed me, dividing the sky no matter which way I turned. Hopeless in the face of this cosmic terror, I fell back on the bed and listened. The harsh, white, trembling scar swayed and settled right in front of my eyes. And nobody but me could see it; there was just a dog somewhere in the distance howling its heart out in a human voice, almost weeping, because nobody would pay attention to what only it knew—or at least *thought* it knew—some vaguely present danger in the darkness.

I remembered that I still hadn't been notified of my wife's death. The fact that no one in Moscow knew my present address didn't mean anything. I was sure that notifications of death are circulated to international organizations, and sooner or later I would be informed through their local offices that she was dead. Or perhaps the notification had been sent, but you know how good the post is these days. It might even have arrived—so much meaningless garbage is sent to new arrivals here, and all in the incomprehensible local language. For all I know, I threw it out with all the other envelopes with their metal staples instead of glue. But that's doubtful. In short, I hadn't received any notification.

As I pulled on a cigarette I noticed a street lamp in the corner of the window. What I had taken for a scar splitting the sky was a band of light reflected from the blinds. I moved my head, and the reflection moved with it. The solution to the riddle calmed me for a second, and I managed to fall asleep.

From that night on I waited not for the notification, but for a letter from her. Again and again in my nightmares I was trying to hide from the steely eyes of people who asked me for my Soviet passport, because I'd snuck into Moscow illegally, and I was my old self again, no different from my old self in any way, until I recalled that I was a foreign citizen and I couldn't go anywhere, not even my family and friends could let me in anywhere, and word of me reached the police, and the insolent smiles and steely glances of denunciation were all around. I used to get up late and then, half-awake, walk around the room for ages, trying to remember what I'd dreamed and why, and where I was.

I would go downstairs, hiding my disillusionment from myself, and make sure that my pigeonhole was empty. It's only temporary, I told myself, I just have to wait until tomorrow. The sunset came quickly and I lay down to sleep again and in my dreams I went back again to the things I couldn't go back to. In this state of half-sleep, or half-wakefulness, I began to write letters. Or rather just one letter, which I kept rewriting. A letter to her. The variations on this one letter were infinite, and they all circled around the same idea, that my life was nothing but a wait at a railway station, that I was waiting for her letter, the way people wait for a train and until it arrived I couldn't do anything but sleep and wait, and until she told me why she didn't come, I couldn't start living. Again and again I reconstructed all the details of our Moscow home from memory, and I could see our bed with the crumpled sheets, and her lying there with her face thrust into the pillow and her cheek resting on her hand. I needed her to lift up her head and smile.

Again and again I fingered the only thing that I had left of her, a handkerchief. I had taken the handkerchief from her open fingers while she lay there motionless with her face turned into the pillow. She must have used it to wipe away her tears and blow her nose all night long. I began carrying the handkerchief with me everywhere. I was never parted from it for a second. When I went to bed, I put it under my pillow. If I were the sort who went in for confessions, I could tell you what I did with that handkerchief when I was alone at night under the blanket and imagined myself tugging the blanket off her and pulling up her nightdress. After a while I stopped changing the bed at all and slept all the time in the sheets that she had ironed with her own hands. The sheets that she had put into the suitcase. The sheets that we had slept in together. I stopped changing my underpants and shirt; I only wore the socks that she had darned before I left. And all the time I kept on composing that one letter to her. Each time I could see new, more distinct details of her clothes, her things, the objects she had touched. Things floated to the surface that I didn't know I'd even seen. And the more the details piled up, the closer her approach seemed to be, but every time I glanced at the band of reflected light stretching across the dark sky in the window, I knew that she was dead and I felt myself tumbling into her absence. It was a black hole in space and time, and I was trying to close it, to patch it with my letters.

I wrote the letters unceasingly, with her handkerchief spread out beside me. Then I would compose her reply to me, and write out a fair copy. Careful copies out of thin air, in her handwriting. I tried to remember every little note she had written, every shopping list. I tried to visualize the notes and then imitate her handwriting as I remembered it. In these "replies," which still sounded a bit like me, she wrote that she had to keep referring to the past, because her present was entirely consumed by my absence. And when she referred to the past, she remembered again that I left her alone in an empty apartment, abandoned her calmly and indifferently, and she could not forgive me for that and she accused me again of betrayal.

In those replies I wrote what I couldn't say to her in my own letter, the things I didn't want to say about myself. That now we had changed places. That now I was the one who kept talking about the importance of intimacy and personal loyalties, while she was the one who couldn't sacrifice her principles. When I received one of these "replies" that nailed me to the bed for the day, I would rip it to shreds. I wanted to cry in despair at the memory of the calm, sleepy indifference on the service-worn face of the border guard with the automatic rifle. Then I started filling the jagged hole in our correspondence with a new reply. Sometimes, when I was woken at night by another new explanation for this unending absurdity, my hand would come across the handkerchief as I searched for a scrap of paper, and I would scrawl the key word onto it so that I would remember it in the morning.

One day, when I unfolded the handkerchief, I saw it was covered all over with my scrawls: from her, from me. Words of persuasion and entreaty, tearful words, angry words, all scrambling over each other, jostling in the confusion of a single letter to an unknown address, and no way of telling who was writing to whom. It was a question and an answer at the same time; she and I were fused into a single being, screeching and demented by the painful cramp of its own guilt.

When I finished writing my letter, I didn't know if I was alive or dead. I can't have eaten anything for days, and I wasn't really sure when it was day and when it was night. I could have gone to see some friends, and I would have been greeted with secret joy at the appearance of another accomplice. They would have looked after me and fed me until I was back on my feet and became one more member added to their union of solidarity. But the very thought of meeting those inquiring glances made me want to stick my head back under the blanket. This was definitely the last letter I had to send, and then everything could go hang; I just had to wait and wait for a reply. I put the letter in an envelope, licked the flap, and squeezed it shut firmly, as though in the hope that nobody but she and I would read the letter. Then I stuck on a stamp with a picture of the Dead Sea and wrote the Moscow address. I put the letter in my breast pocket and went out.

The local post office was closed so I got on the bus to go to the main one. But in the bus either hunger or the gas fumes made me feel sick, so I got out at the central bus station to walk the rest of the way to the center. I was walking past carpenters' shops and metalworkers' shops, and the sound of the hammers banging built up into a constant crescendo of noise centered around my temples, probably fused with the beating of my heart, and my lips began mockingly whispering a Soviet ditty about metalsmiths who forge the keys of happiness into a steel breast containing a flaming engine instead of a heart. Then that last conversation about one's place of residence began circling around in my brain. Did you have to be the person you were born as, or did you have to be someone who didn't exist?

The pounding of the hammers became unbearable, and I turned into the side alleys. I almost floated along the streets, which further away from the bus routes became hundreds of separate little cities. Like any other part of Jerusalem, they didn't seem entirely real because people lived in each of these cities, not for the sake of passing their lives there, but in order to prove to every passerby that their lives were different from anyone else's, the genuine article. I'd obviously walked to the eastern quarter of the city. There was already an evening chill in the air, and handfuls of Arab workers walked by in their plaster-stained pants and white keffiyehs without noticing me. In their keffiyehs, and with their shalwars too, they looked a bit like women coming out of a steambath, towels wound around their heads. Everyone here was naked and defenseless. I moved out from the wall and almost collided with a priest in a black cassock, carrying a suitcase. He had been stopped by a lady in a short skirt, also carrying a suitcase, and they talked rapidly for a while, and then they laughed, and the woman, still laughing, hurried off in one direction, while the priest turned into a side alley and glanced at me as if he were inviting me to follow. I went on past the Jaffa Gate, past the four palm trees that look so absurd in this city, and then down again until I found myself here in this quarter. I walked along a street with big empty houses and gas fumes and the smell of engine oil. And there were the hammers pounding once again.

And then I saw a portrait of Theodore Herzl in a window. It was a very strange surprise in this quarter of the city to see the portrait of the father of Zionism that was once long ago shown to me in secret in Moscow. If you look across the street, you can see it in the shop window opposite. But of course, it's dark now. When I went up to the window with the photographs, it was just beginning to get dark.

The house belonged to the grandsons of the man Theodore Herzl stayed with when he arrived in Jerusalem to seek a meeting with Kaiser Wilhelm, who was also here at the time, though it's not really clear why the kaiser came here. There were no rooms to be had in any decent hotel, and the prophet of the world's first Jewish state was bitten by bedbugs in the room he did eventually get. He wanted to move away from the bedbugs, but all the hotels were packed because of Kaiser Wilhelm's arrival. Then Theodore was offered a room in this house on Mammila Street. When Theodore Herzl went off to meet Kaiser Wilhelm, the grandfather lent him his top hat. A top hat was absolutely required. Without the top hat, we wouldn't have this first state of ours. In the English note for tourists in the window it was said that one of the walls in the house museum was left unplastered, and I couldn't understand what it was all about, until I figured out from the stream of words that leaving a wall unplastered was a way of commemorating the destruction of the temple.

I remembered that when I left Moscow I still hadn't papered one of the walls in the corridor. When we were decorating, the wallpaper ran out and we covered one of the walls in the corridor with pictures from the magazine *America*. We kept intending to buy the extra wallpaper, but we never got round to it. I had to open the door again with my key. I had to see that unpapered wall again. And it suddenly hit me that leaving a wall unplastered was the most terrible reminder of a deserted house. I dreamed of a bright temple built on separation and tears. I wouldn't have been surprised if they'd left one wall not just unplastered, but unbuilt, and left the house with one wall missing, so that the wind would always blow in and remind you that your home is not here. That you are only a guest in this world, and someday you will go home.

How did those men feel who were driven out of Jerusalem, where they were born? They swore solemnly to themselves not to fall in love with the new foreign land where they found asylum. They were always preparing to hurry back, and their suitcases were always at the ready. They greedily sought out the latest news about Jerusalem: Power would change hands any moment now, and they would pack their suitcases and open the door with the key again and they would talk over and over again about seeing again what they had left behind, every detail with a meaning that only they knew. And the children began to write down this song of homecoming, and their fathers invented laws so that every detail could be remembered, so that the old routes would not become confused when the time of homecoming came. All of the laws, from the washing of hands to the sequence of daily readings from the books, are just a crazy song of nostalgia for a place once walked through and now walked through only in dreams, and these dreams need to be written down carefully.

But then another generation was born, and for them the laws became a science; they begin fishing for pristine truth in this shorthand record, and drawing philosophical conclusions from the telephone directory, and organizing debates on postmarks. After all, the laws were composed by exchange of letters, an uninterrupted correspondence with those few left behind in Jerusalem. An uninterrupted exchange of questions and answers, questions and answers by post, and between question and answer years passed, because a letter was sent during one empire and the reply was received when Jerusalem was already under the sway of a different empire. And only a few individuals began gradually to understand that the homecoming was being confined more and more within the bounds of an envelope, that the suitcases had split and collapsed long ago, that it was impossible to go back to the place you never came from. Instead, you always returned to yourself, and all that was left was the weary longing for a homecoming.

Everyone who has ever gone away spends his own life justifying himself to those left behind and to himself for transgressing the final commandment of faithfulness: be killed, but do not part. And most who return to Jerusalem cannot forgive themselves for having survived. The one who believes in the fatefulness of his flight will not return. He will wait until his prayers change the world. Those who return are those who were ready to die before: You have to live where you have already died.

But then pupils of the pupils appeared, and they mistakenly fell in love with the fate of others. They began to live with grief that was not their own, a grief for things that they had not lost. You can't experience someone else's exile as your own. Did you ever have an affair with someone else's wife? With the wife of your friend and teacher—when you want, but you can't, and you can, but you don't want to. It's the stolen pleasure you have dreamed about all your life. But you have the feeling that in robbing him, you are robbing yourself, because you are almost his creation. That's what happens with God and the homeland when your homeland belongs only to God and no one else, if you understand what I mean. How many suicides will there be out of love for one's father's wife, a woman who is not and will never become part of your family? You are not her son. But neither is she your stepmother.

And then, in the middle of my meditations, there was a voice: "Young man, young man!" I suddenly heard a woman call out behind me. The slightly husky and homely voice sounded so familiar that I didn't turn round straightaway, thinking it must belong to me or my invisible partner in conversation. When I did turn around, through the gathering dusk were the brightly lit window and the open doors of a diner on the other side of the street. As you've probably guessed, it was this very diner where we are sitting now. If only I hadn't turned around, simply gone on my way, thinking I'd imagined that voice. But I did turn around. I saw the brightly lit doorway and the window here, and I was drawn to the cozy light like a moth to a lamp. I set off, staggering, across the road and saw a woman waving to me from the doorway: "Young man, young man!" For a second I thought she was someone I'd known for a long time, but I couldn't remember where from, and for that second I was somewhere else; time suddenly swung and drifted, and I squeezed my eyes tight to shake off the dizziness. When I half-opened them again, the woman was coming out of the diner and beckoning to me. "Can you help me carry this suitcase to the main post office?" she asked with a mixture of trite female coquetry and genuine entreaty.

At once I recalled my own reason for being here on this street: I had to send a letter to my wife. Why couldn't this woman carry her own junk for herself, why didn't she think about it earlier? I thought angrily. The smell of roasting meat and hot soup made me feel dizzy and sick again. She looked at me with sympathetic concern. She could have been my mother. She was well over fifty, perhaps even older. It was hard to tell in the twilight outside. Her lips were brightly painted, and she wore an absurdly coquettish beret on her head. She was like some important bureaucrat's widow trying to look younger than her age, like those charitable ladies who fight their own boredom by investigating the digs of new arrivals, peeking into their refrigerators and proffering the confused advice of an old hand on how to save two lira in a grocery store on the other side of town by spending four to get there.

I took a look at the suitcase standing beside her. It was probably stuffed full of used clothes for new arrivals. Always they wanted you to change your clothes. Do you remember the story about the Russian aristocrat who left Russia because he had quarreled with the tsar? He supposedly took off all his clothes at the border and left the country naked. I reluctantly took hold of the suitcase and swayed as I tried to lift it. "There, you see, you see, I've always said that at your age it's very important to follow a strict regime, you need to eat properly and get plenty of sleep at night," she rattled off, and took hold of the suitcase from the other side. Both of us clutching the same large leather handle, we set off downhill for the post office.

The suitcase was awkward to carry. It banged against my legs, and her wide hips pushed on it from the left, but I couldn't take it on my own. We walked on and on, and the walk seemed so long that I began to think we would never get to the post office. I even wondered if we were really going there. Sometimes she would turn her head and look at me with that look of sympathy and irritating concern, but I didn't have the strength to get angry and drop the suitcase. She seemed like a punishment I had to bear, and I simply grimaced as I felt the ache in my shoulder grow stronger and my arm grow weaker. But she kept glancing at me, and I tried to hold myself up straight and make sure I didn't stumble or fall, because I had to carry this burden all the way no matter what, although sometimes the thought did come to me that nobody had forced me to carry the suitcase and I could refuse there and then on some polite pretext—but there I was carrying God knows what, God knows where, God knows why.

The crowds on the streets grew thicker, and it seemed as though it was some kind of holiday, a carnival. We wove around cars at intersections through which they in turn slowly made their way through the crowd. The fierce mirth of helplessness drove me on. The air all around was filled with colorful rattles and whistles and everyone, old and young, was waving little plastic hammers. Grownups and children jostled each other, overtook each other, leaned out of the windows of a bus to bang the heads of unsuspecting pedestrians. But the blows were not for real; the plastic hammer came down with an unpleasant squeak, as though someone had stepped on a frog, or a mouse had got caught in a trap. The squeaking and the dull rumbling mingled with the shouts and the laughter into a single hubbub, through which I could hear the shrill voice of the owner of the suitcase. Everyone made way for her in a gesture of inexplicable respect, so that we walked through a constantly evolving empty space in the crowd.

"You're really in a bad way, I suppose nobody's taking care of you, you need to be set back on your feet, I suppose you're all on your own, banging your head against the wall and imagining that the wall is reality," she twittered as I recall. "You should blend in with the festival, but you haven't even got the strength to smile, because you carry on living in a different world—the old one. You ought to connect your present day with a new circle of people, and become a fully active member of society, don't you see? When I came to this country many years ago, who could ever have imagined that someday there would be crowds like this on the streets? My husband came on his own first, but I refused point-blank, I cried without stopping for a whole year while he showered me with letters trying to persuade me and begging me to come. At first I was dying to go back to Moscow, then I got used to it here: Time heals everything, all those sorrows and woes; the main thing is to stop comparing your present life with the past, to become part of a new team, don't you agree?"

I tried to force a smile; she preached so ardently, like a Komsomol leader from the twenties. The little hammers were squeaking in my ears and I remembered the saying that the devil cannot touch the ground of the Holy Land, so he makes his home in the heads of the people. And on holidays they probably beat each other over the head to drive out the devil. The pounding began once again round my temples, and it mingled with the memory of heavy workers' hands pounding with their hammers that afternoon on that street. Finally the long gray building of the post office with the black gun hole windows rose up uncertainly ahead of us and we were walking along the sidewalk to the entrance, with the crowd still making way for us. I was very dizzy, and I mechanically registered the absence of the bored guard who usually chewed sunflower seeds instead of checking bags for terrorist bombs. The doors were locked. "We can't be too late, surely?" said the woman, letting go of the handle and throwing her hands up in the air in surprise. The suitcase was left hanging in my single hand for a second, and then it fell to the asphalt with a heavy thud, and I fainted.

When I came round the first thing I saw was a pair of woman's legs with sharp knees. She was squatting beside me and daubing my forehead with a wet handkerchief. "Hunger, you obviously fainted from hunger." Her voice sounded like it was being poured through cotton wool. "You have to be fed immediately, and then put straight to bed. As soon as we get home I'll take care of you." She helped me to my feet.

The suitcase had come open and a heap of the letters had spilled out. White envelopes scattered over the black asphalt. A crowd was gathering around us. I felt dizzy. There was something indecent and criminal about the scattered envelopes, about the whole scene, and although I didn't sense any embarrassment in her behavior (in fact it seemed as though everyone here knew her and was not in the least surprised), I fought off my dizziness and helped her stuff the letters back into the suit-case. And even in that condition, when I could scarcely believe my own eyes, I was immediately struck by the inscription in standard lettering on the envelopes: "Notification of Death." The same words stamped on every envelope: "Notification of Death." On another, and another, on all of them. Bizarre. But I was in no condition to feel surprise. "You'll get a good rest at my place and the chance to stop worrying about all these prob-lems," she continued in a persuasive voice, then she snapped the suitcase closed and picked it up with one hand so easily that I wondered why on earth she had needed my help in the first place.

"I live alone, I buried my husband ages ago, you'll have peace and quiet. And please don't object, don't imagine this is charity—I've been looking for the right person for a long time now," she protested, although I hadn't said a word. "You write a bit, don't you? I can find some fairly easy work for you to do—you just need to copy out a few things, but I'll tell you all about that later, now let's get home as quickly as possible."

She carried on talking in the same tone of dictatorial care, like a nurse, but I wasn't listening, or rather I accepted what she said as a given fact that I had already come to terms with long before; I was so far beyond caring what would happen to me, I felt as though everything that could happen to me already had. She gently prodded me on, and as we set off I heard a laugh behind me, as someone nearby could no longer restrain himself and hit me on the head with his little hammer. I hardly felt the blow—it was like a light tap from the palm of a hand—but when I heard the squeak, it was as though something inside me burst, and suddenly there were tears pouring from my eyes, pouring down as I silently wept. I was weeping for the man who imagined that he lived in defiance or in the name of truth and was suddenly made to realize quite clearly that he was a weak-willed nonentity who lived at the expense of others' suffering. He thought he was being branded and persecuted, but he was actually tolerated out of a sense of charity, like the family idiot.

She held me by the hand and didn't seem to notice that I was crying. We walked along a street that led upward and the crowd made way for us again, either in fright or in amazement at the sight of such a strange pair. We walked as far as the market, when she turned in through the iron gates. The market was empty at night, with rows of empty stalls receding into the distance where there were locks on the doors of the warehouses dotting dark passageways leading off God knows where, and only the light from the occasional swaying lamp lighting up a sudden corner. The sound of talking and singing and laughter from the main street echoed from one end of the market to the other, bounced off the corners and the gates, and the market seemed still alive in the clamoring shadows cast by the yellow lamps as she led me through it with the certainty of a blind man who knows the way by heart. Then we emerged from the echoing dead voices and she went through an archway, and inside there was not just a yard, but an entire network of side streets all squeezed into the same quarter, crammed with houses, and more houses, and still more houses after that. The houses had thick walls, and the walls had gates in them, but the gates didn't lead into yards, they led into further labyrinths of side streets, and when I looked up I saw the dark crowns of trees against the sky and stairways leading up to the second level of dwellings, and they ended in archways, and no doubt beyond those archways there were more cities within the city, and there was no way I would ever find my way back out through these cities with their sealed stone walls ready for an enemy siege.

She suddenly stopped under one of the arches, put down the suitcase, and began rummaging purposefully in her hand-bag. Finally she pulled out not your average assortment of keys but a long metal thing, and began fumbling with it in an almost invisible lock in the wall of the archway. Eventually the lock clicked, and she took it off its metal rings. As she did this, the odd key slipped from her grasp and clattered against the stones. When I bent down to pick it up, it gleamed for a second in the light from a street lamp, and I saw it was the broken handle from a brass Turkish coffeepot. She took this strange substitute for a key out of my hand, smiled apologetically, then opened the door and pushed me inside. I screwed up my eyes, expect-ing blinding light after the dark night outside, but when I opened them again, the light was strangely familiar: It was that light you get when you switch on the lamp at dawn or when it's already so bright outside that you don't need a light. I took a step forward and almost slipped. The floor was unexpectedly smooth, like a mirror; in fact it was a mirror. I looked around and I saw my reflection on the walls too, because they were mir-rors as well; I couldn't tell whether I was walking forward or someone was walking toward me, or how many people there were in the room, how many doors there were, or how to get out and how to get in. I tried to go straight to the couch by the table in the corner, but when I set off toward the corner, trying hard not to slip, I immediately banged my head against a mirror wall. "Not that way, come back here," said the owner of the suitcase, with a rippling laugh. "My husband was used to a big flat in Moscow, so he covered the walls and the floor with mirrors to make it seem like we had a whole suite and not just one room." She took me by the elbow, led me over to the red couch, and sat me down, moving the table up so close to me that even if I wasn't exhausted it would have been hard for me to get up from where I sat with my knees high in the air so that I would have had to push very hard on the floor in order to get up anyway, and of course the floor was slippery as hell.

"Now we'll have some soup, soup, soupy soup." She smacked me on the cheek as a mother would a little kid, then tossed off her high-heeled shoes, put on some slippers, and darted with frightening agility to the other end of the room. She slid along in a series of smooth movements, moving her legs as though she were on skates. Her reflection in the walls and the ceiling set my head spinning again. She opened a cupboard in the wall and began taking out packets and jars and bags and little bottles, then she took a quick sniff at the contents under the corks and the rubber stoppers and set everything out in front of a huge saucepan. She filled it up to the brim with water and began sprinkling and mixing and working away with a ladle and various spoons, and then sprinkling some more, and tasting and blowing with her lips pursed up, and clouds of steam began rising from the saucepan, and a rich, enchanting aroma that reminded me of every delicious thing in the world began to fill the room as she stood there leaning over the saucepan, slowly swirling the ladle in the soup.

The foam rose for a third time when she finally set the huge plate of steaming soup in front of me. The forgotten sensation of ravenous hunger must have confused me, because I attacked it immediately and burnt my lips, and my hand was trembling as I raised the spoon to my mouth. She sat opposite me and watched me with glowing eyes, following every spoonful. When I happened to look up for a second and met her gaze, I blushed, but then I smiled and went back to the wonderful soup. When I reached the bottom of the plate I mopped up the remaining beans or lentils or whatever with a piece of bread. Every spoonful of that soup had a simultaneously relaxing and invigorating effect, and when I finished it, for the first time in months I felt a healthy drowsiness weighing down my head and my eyelids. I stretched out on the couch and closed my eyes with a smile.

I felt as though my drowsy body was flooded with that enveloping, scorching strength that comes when you come into the house from the frost, and the stove is already red-hot. Your body starts to relax, and the steady warmth penetrates your skin as you gradually begin to feel every bit of your body as a whole. I hadn't felt that way for years. The aches and the fatigue passed, together with that gnawing uncertainty that made me toss and turn in bed at night. I raised my eyelids for a moment and noted with blissful indifference that I was floating in a hot bath, and the smell of soap bubbles reminded me of my childhood, when gentle, familiar hands rinsed me off and stroked my body, undisturbed by any of its shortcomings, and I laughed at this pleasant tickling and stretched from my toes to the top of my head in a single movement of relaxing readiness. At first I was worried that I was forgetting what I couldn't remember, what could never have happened but which I believed in, believing it was impossible that anything irreparable had happened. But then I forgot even this.

My eyes opened to a room that was lit up, not by the morning light, nor electric light, but rather by a pervasive incandescence. I was stretched out on the couch wearing a huge, soft dressing gown. I saw myself reflected on the ceiling, and in a drowsy yet somehow wakeful state slowly looked down to find her leaning over me, her head at my feet and her lips scorching their way swiftly over my skin. Her robe came open and her long legs spread above my face; our bodies got entangled. The red tongue between her thighs, wide and trembling, slid over my lips as I sank into her mouth and, with a final shudder, sank back into oblivion.

Once again a gentle hand supported me as I floated on waves of warm water. The soap bubbles were like the snow of my childhood, and then I was back lying on the same red couch, wrapped in the expansive dressing gown, and my hostess rubbed my body until it glowed all over. She sat beside me, half-naked, looking somehow younger, and I looked with pleasure at her smooth, strong face with the wide-open eyes that gazed straight at me, smiling slyly without the slightest embarrassment. Suddenly I stopped noticing her wrinkles and the folds of skin under her chin; I stopped noticing the age difference. In fact, I failed to find difference anywhere. As if by magic, everything was familiar once again and there was nothing to regret. Everything was still to come. Everything was already over. A dream within a dream, in which I dreamt only of taking a half-step forward and then sliding back, and every second expanded into a lifetime and the whole of life fit easily into a single day.

I looked at her with devoted gratitude. I looked tenderly at her large aging breasts peeping out of her open dressing gown, and I wanted to reach out with my lips, like a child. I pulled her onto myself, throwing the dressing gown open, and rolled her onto her back. But she whispered that we shouldn't and put her admonishing finger to my lips. I drew her palm to my mouth and kissed it, and she wriggled because it tickled. And then: "How about some coffee? Why don't we have some coffee-coff-coff-coffee, ah?" I nodded and she slid away on her flip-flop skates and once again I was amazed at how lightly she moved, but even that seemed familiar, because I couldn't remember where and when we met, but I knew that I had been here a long time and I liked it. She made a turn round the stove and then came over to the table and set the Turkish coffeepot in front of me. She set it down carefully, because the handle was broken off, and wrapped a towel around it. We drank the coffee slowly, and with each hot mouthful my head felt lighter and clearer, without any burden on my conscience. The old habit of making conversation over coffee drove me to try to remember something important, but I couldn't remember anything, and my anxiety obviously began to show in my eyes, because at that moment she took my hand and warmed it on her breast, and I forgot that I should remember anything at all.

"Well now, shall we get down to work?" she asked at last as she cleared the cups from the table. I nodded, watching her movements in rapture. She slid over to the end of the room and came back with the immense suitcase that I had already forgotten about; I was seeing it for the very first time. "Ever since I haven't had my husband here with me, I've had to carry the full burden myself. Now you'll see what I mean," she said, scooping a heap of envelopes out of the suitcase. "I can tell you here and now that you won't regret it. It's creative work. But the main thing is, it's rewarding. It's work that our descendants will remember. Let me explain. A husband has left his wife. A great misfortune, you must agree. But what if the husband didn't want to leave his wife, but was forced to? A double misfortune, wouldn't you say? He was forced to leave her by circumstances beyond his control, and she, in turn, wasn't able to join him because of those same circumstances, despite their mutual devotion, fidelity, and love. I don't have to explain it to you, do I?"

But I didn't understand what she was hinting at, so I went on rapturously listening to her. She sorted out the envelopes and went on: "I'm talking about the wives of men who emigrate. The wives who stay behind. When the husband has to leave his home and country to go to his historic homeland. And procrastination is worse than death. It is better to die traveling than sitting behind prison bars. Of course, there are opportunities for heroism everywhere, but not everywhere is there a place for you. And knowing that Russia will not let anyone back in, that there is no way back to Russia, many are obliged to overcome their human affections and leave their wives behind. Some wives have sick parents, some have bad hearts, some know state secrets. But letters know no boundaries. On both sides of the Iron Curtain there are people writing letters to each other, and this association by correspondence becomes a new life in common and gives the woman hope that nothing has changed and that in just a little while she will join her husband in their marital bed, and her children will embrace their father."

She adjusted the dressing gown at her breast prudishly. "So you see, armed with the incontrovertible facts of implacable hatred for separation, our agency does everything possible to permit the wife who has been abandoned perforce to join her husband, even despite the fact that her husband is already dead. Yes, dead. We continue his life's work, the goal of which is that he and his wife and their children and their grandchildren should not die among aliens, but in their own historical homeland." Again she adjusted the dressing gown. "We have a network of full-time agents, but so far we have only been able to cover the Jerusalem region, and we can't really manage that. People die too often in Jerusalem: sudden changes in the weather, terrorist bombs, simple depression. A man pulls up his roots and takes the great leap, tearing himself away from his own past, and often he stumbles and falls, a long fall from the height of his newly acquired freedom when he is left without his accustomed supports. And the wives are left without letters. We have taken on the work of continuing their correspondence. Whenever a Russian émigré dies, our agent, who is in daily contact with the undertakers and the morgues, immediately gathers all the available information about him, from biographical texts to small intimate habits, and if he was alone and no one else knows about him, he is added to our list of permanent correspondents. When we have received full information about him from our agent in one of these envelopes, we accept the voluntary obligation of continuing his correspondence with his wife or family in Russia."

Noticing the confusion in my eyes, she hurried on. "It's not

nearly as impossible as it seems at first. We carry on the correspondence with his wife in his name, copying his handwriting,
correlating our letters with his wife's, carrying on writing even
when we don't get a reply: Who knows how the censor works,
and what it lets through and what it doesn't? I'm sure you grasp
something of the unusual and difficult, but exceptionally hon-
orable nature of this work? Will you be able to imitate someone
else's handwriting?" I nodded in hasty enthusiasm. I should
think so! One thing I had never had in all my life was my own
handwriting. So since the time I wrote my very first word, I had
been forced to imitate someone or another. In school I copied
my teacher's handwriting. That was just the beginning: When I
had to write anything by hand, I first thought of someone who
would write something of the kind, and then I painstakingly
imitated that person's handwriting. But when I copied his
handwriting, I heard the intonations of his voice in my mind,
so that everything I wrote seemed to be dictated by that person's voice. In all my life I hadn't really expressed a single
thought of my own. And that would probably be useful in this
highly responsible work. She smiled approvingly at me. I would
have done anything to deserve that look.

"I can see from your eyes that you are capable of entering
unreservedly into the lives of every person who has died in this
holy part of the world, every person who has sacrificed his life
to the idea of dying in his historic homeland. So let's not drag
things out, let's get started." And she began sorting out
envelopes.

We got started. It was easy and quite clear. First I studied
the contents of the envelope sent by the agent and experi-
mented with the person's handwriting on a separate piece of
paper. Then when I had mastered their curlicues and flourishes,

it was quite simple for me to write a letter to the wife far away filled with details of daily life, the prospects for building the new life, ideas and opinions, proclamations of eternal love, and vows of eternal fidelity. I eventually felt that I had lost myself completely in this world of other people's names, that I had disappeared and been relieved of my own name and the sense of anything I might have to do on my own behalf. I stopped worrying about my own fate, my devotion, and the menacing sequence of the days, jangling like so many links of a chain. I stopped worrying that with every passing day something disappeared that wouldn't make it as far as today. I stopped worrying about my past without a future and my tomorrow without a day before yesterday, when today was a black hole in my head. Unhappiness is a sense of loss, but I had nothing to lose. The people I encountered through letters were of different generations, but they existed simultaneously as I sat there, each of them repeating my own fate while I repeated someone else's. You see, I was fortunate enough to encounter in someone else's life what I thought could not be understood in my own. I had stumbled into that moment when one stands in someone else's shoes and sees himself from the outside, spits over his left shoulder, and gives up on everything.

My eyes grew misty when I thought of this intimate stranger who was someone else's wife: I always pictured her sitting by a lamp, leaning over my letter, pressing a handkerchief to her eyes, and then reading the letter in a joyful voice to her children and loved ones. I lost all sense of time. The letters were easy to deal with. Eventually the agency information began to repeat itself, the biographies of the dead men and their relations with their wives were all pretty much the same, and so after a certain point my letters began to repeat themselves, and it was as though I was writing the same letter all the time, constantly improving it in the process of perpetual repetition. Again and again I ran away from the shameful historical complicity by way of sacrificing daily intimacy; again and again I tried to find tangible justifications for my departure in the positive aspects of life here. Again and again I reviewed my life as a kind of transitional period in an approach to the ideal, and all the irredeemable misfortunes of my days were only isolated and atypical occurrences in an overall optimistic picture.

When she got up, my hostess would discuss with me what I had written and make some slight corrections, which became less significant each time, and then she took her huge black suitcase and went off to collect the new notifications of death. I never knew when the morning or the evening came, because the blinds were always closed and the same lighting was always on. Every time she closed the door after her, she wagged her finger at me in mock threat, telling me to make myself at home, and this made me smile, because I couldn't remember any other home except this one.

I didn't understand, though, her only request: not to go into the next room, which was closed off by a door under which a slipper had been stuffed to keep it from banging in a draft. The door was directly opposite the table where I wrote my letters, so it was constantly tempting my eye. Sometimes, when I was exhilarated by my own inspiration, as I strode around the table, my instinctive curiosity caused me to absent-mindedly take hold of the door handle, but I would always remember her warning and pull back my hand before any damage was done. Still, as I pulled my hand away and thought about my next hero's letter, I would suddenly feel that I had to remember what I'd promised myself to forget, and my hand would reach out again toward the door. But whenever I was really about to pull it open, my hostess would return, come sliding over to me, take me by the hand, and lead me back to the table.

At those moments I'd feel the vaguest kind of annoyance well up inside me at the sight of her tall, smart figure with the suitcase. I was ashamed of my inward annoyance: I owed her everything. She did everything for me, she had saved me from the danger that I couldn't remember, but I knew for certain had existed. She'd take me by the hand and sit me down on the red couch. I'd feel suddenly dizzy and weak. Have I mentioned that she grew younger with every day? With perfect regularity I would feel the pangs of a fierce, tormenting hunger, and she would prepare more of her fantastic soup. It spread a warm fire through my belly that cheered me and relaxed me, and I would fall into that sweet slumber and feel her moist, captivating kisses on every inch of my body, and the feeling inside me grew and swelled up until there was nothing left except the unrestrained need to swallow her with my own mouth, and we moved together in a single culminating spasm of desire to leap beyond the bounds of our own skin. Then she would bring coffee again, carrying the jezvah in a towel, and like a new man I would smooth away the final traces of concern and enthusiastically go back to writing letters. I was approaching perfection—epistolary perfection, that is.

One day she set a new address in front of me. This time my new name apparently covered an entire generation in its complexity: The man was called Theodore Elisier ben Gurion

Trumpeldor. "Our most honored client," she told me in a hoarse voice, "and our favorite," she added with a strange smile. The agent's notes said that he was a qualified obstetrician, but never actually practiced, unless you count his role in the birth of his own nation. While still in Russia, he was one of the major figures in the revival of the language of his prehistoric ancestors. He could rattle off the names of his ancestors by heart, and believed that everyone speaks the language of somebody's ancestors. So when people spoke to him in a language that didn't belong to his own ancestors, he pretended not to hear them. Since neither his aged parents nor his wife spoke the language of their prehistoric ancestors, he eventually stopped speaking to anyone in the family circle: First he pretended that he couldn't hear, and then he really did stop listening. He began communicating with his eyes and with gestures, and then finally he left his wife and family and moved to Jerusalem.

As an officer in the Russian army, he had lost an eye and a leg in the Japanese war, and this experience led to his developing the battle tactics and strategy that were named in his honor: "right eye and wrong foot combat." Throughout his life he worked on a mammoth project—bringing electricity to the gigantic desert to the south so that even in the dark of night he would be able see what a huge expanse of virgin territory there was for settling the assimilated elements, as they were called at the time. He was killed under strange circumstances, by terrorists who wanted to settle the land with different elements. There was a hill named after him that can be found on any map.

I was inspired as I set about continuing the discussion with his widow, who had stayed in Russia. He wrote almost nothing about his private life, and she simply wasn't there in his letters, because he had devoted all his life to the ideas of electrifying the language and the wilderness. "We must become the nuts and the bolts of the new life," he wrote, when he finally grasped the essence of the matter. "Our lives must be guided through and through by the future, which must look like that tasty carrot that is hung before the nose of a donkey to urge him into motion. This future is in our ancestors' past." It felt like I had rediscovered the indivisible unity between myself and the world around me.

The only thing that hindered my epistolary imagination in its flight was my handwriting. I seemed finally to have developed my own style, and it was crooked, with shaky letters, and sometimes the pen skidded and the letters went askew: I tried copying it out again, but it was no better. It was obviously an old man's sclerotic writing, but my hostess said that was just what we needed, because that was exactly how Theodore Elisier ben Gurion Trumpeldor used to write. From that moment on she stayed home more than usual, and would end up spending whole days sitting with me.

It turned out that she had an entire archive of his photographs, old newspapers with articles by him and about him, his open letters to friends and comrades-in-arms. She became involved in the work of composing letters to his widow. She sat opposite me, looking younger than ever, wrapped in her dressing gown. It happened more than once when looking through the old newspapers for articles about him that I would find one or two holes carefully cut out. "Why are there holes in the newspapers?" I asked her once. "Jealousy," she said, blushing, "jealousy and vanity—qualities any genuine statesman has to have. He was jealous and vain, and when anybody criticized him publicly, he carefully cut it out of the papers. It's a crime against history, of course, but then we ourselves are the makers of history. I can only tell you that he was a genuine historical warrior. We are all here now despite the natural course of history. He understood that quite literally. Perhaps that was what drove him mad before he died. He was killed for standing above history: During the last days of his life he went around town with his hands in the air announcing that he was a utility pole carrying the lines of our electric future. He was a brilliant man," she went on, tears gleaming in her eyes. My mind flashed the shadow of a forgotten question.

"Did you know him?" I asked her after a long pause.

"Good grief, wasn't it obvious to you from the very beginning? He was my husband," she said calmly, looking past me into empty space. "Of course at first it was impossible for me to forgive him for going away, leaving me while I slept. But it was my fault, after all. I used to be an actress, and my life consisted of the stage and the various masks I wore on it. He went from being my husband to a stranger who spoke in some funny gobbledegook. I didn't realize then that he was a midwife of the new life. But he showered me with letters, and in time I cast off the mask. It was a waste of time acting and playing the hypocrite on stage, when the new theater of life, lit up with his electricity, was waiting for me down here. So I came to join him. But it was too late. He'd been killed the day before I got here. There's a good reason for why the light is always on in this room. It's a memorial to his cause, to his life's work. It's my inspiration. I collected everything I could find about him. I copied out articles by hand in a special album, an album that

sums up his life. I missed having his letters so much. By copying out old letters from him, it was as though I received them
again. That was how I got the idea for our agency. And since
you've been here, carrying out this work with such devotion,
giving it all your energy, I wondered why I shouldn't let myself
receive letters from him again—from the other side, you see?"
I began to understand, but not completely. That forgotten
dizziness was creeping back. She sat there looking at me with
blind affection in her eyes, and I sat there seeing her through
eyes clouded by nausea, slowly engaging in the struggle to
remember how I wound up with this buxom old failed actress.

You can probably imagine what I was feeling, when you
suddenly stop and realize that you've been here before and this
has happened to you before. In another life. And you can see
your life, but you don't realize that you're dreaming it, and you
try to understand how you got to where you are, somewhere
where you shouldn't be. It was as if she was looking at me in an
old photograph. I looked at my unfinished letter, written in
crooked, uneven writing. It was my handwriting. I looked over
at the pile of newspapers. I was again struck by the likeness to a
face I had seen once; perhaps it was her face, when I first met
her. When did I first meet her? How long ago?

There had to be something somewhere. Something to put
my finger on, some clue, some proof, that I was not him, and
she was not her. She took out a handkerchief to dry her eyes.
She was clutching it in her trembling hands. "The handkerchief!" The word spun round and round in my head. The handkerchief was what had been missing. I thrust my hand into my
pocket. The thing I'd carried around for as long as I could
remember wasn't there. But it wouldn't have been in this pocket

anyway, you see, because it was in the pocket of that dressing gown, and I hadn't always worn the dressing gown. So, where were my own clothes?

I quickly scanned the room, went over to the coat rack, which had nothing hanging on it but her beret. I plodded back to the couch and looked behind it. But I couldn't make out anything in the dim light of the room. I thrust my arm down behind the couch and tried to reach the floor. Suddenly something ran over my hand, tickling it. I pulled it back in disgust and saw a small spider scurry across the plush material and hide. There was a cobweb on my palm, and I rubbed my hand squeamishly on the dressing gown. So there were spiders here!

"What are you looking for?" she asked, watching me with a frightened expression. I didn't answer and went on rummaging through the place. I moved the furniture, betraying the other cobwebs in the room, as I threw aside one item after another in disgust. I felt dizzy, though, and the floor was slippery such that moving this insubstantial furniture required immense effort and cost me an enormous amount of energy. The dust got into my eyes. My vision was impaired. She just sat there watching me, muttering something in her confusion as I began methodically upending everything in the room, from the furniture to the saucepans. I tossed the coffeepot with the broken handle, then picked it up and actually looked inside. I found the old coffee grounds. Another small spider crawled by. I was almost sick. I tore the upholstery on the couch and bedbugs spilled out in a terrifying multitude, like an army of servants defending their mistress.

"What's wrong with you, what are you looking for, there is nothing here to look for," she babbled.

"Give me back my handkerchief," I said coldly.

"What handkerchief?" she asked, hiding the hand with the handkerchief in the pocket of her dressing gown.

"Stop this," I demanded, my hand still held out. "You know what I'm talking about. Give it back to me, you bitch. Give me that handkerchief, my wife's handkerchief," I said, remembering at last.

"But it's my handkerchief," she said coyly as she waved it in the air. "It always was mine. And I've no idea what wife you're talking about. We've been married for ages." She held out her arms to me.

Shrieking madly, I darted toward her to grab the handkerchief that she was now holding above her head, teasing me like a dog. She moved aside and I slipped and fell on my hands and knees. Then I noticed the door in the wall, the door jammed shut with the slipper. She caught the direction of my gaze, and just as I had got halfway to my feet and put my hand on the door handle and all I had to do was push the door, she jerked me by the shoulders with such force that I was sent sliding across the room. I crawled toward her and tried again to grab the handkerchief. She squirmed away and we slid around on the floor.

Somehow she managed again to slip away from me, with her outstretched hand clutching the handkerchief, mocking me. My body was aching as though I'd been performing circus tricks. I was beginning to feel exhausted. Then she pounced, threw me over onto my back, sat on top of me, and covered the top half of my face with the handkerchief.

"You little fool, do you know how many years I waited for you?" I heard her say in a choking whisper, and her lips began wandering over my body. I couldn't lift up my head; she had pulled the handkerchief tight over it and was pressing it down against the floor with both hands. I heard her strained whisper again: "Now we can do it, now's the very time, because our time is coming to an end." And I felt her hand fumbling under my dressing gown, her long plump legs grasping my legs, thrusting them upward beneath her. Her lips were crushing mine again, her swollen nipples rubbed against my chest, and her full belly pressed me against the floor. "Don't hurry, now, don't hurry," she murmured, biting my lips, and she slowly mounted me with smooth sliding movements. The last thing I heard was a hissing whisper that scorched my ear: "Don't take it out, don't take it out of the envelope."

When I came to, she was gone. My body was in pain. I felt sick. The light that only seconds before had seemed eternal was now a dim depressing bronze glow. She was nowhere to be seen; her suitcase had disappeared along with the rest of her things. I could just barely hear a suppressed sighing. At first I thought it might just be the buzzing in my head. I sat up unsteadily and crawled toward the table, but the floor was no longer slippery and there were no more multiple reflections, as though the mirrors had somehow been extinguished. When I reached the table I collapsed onto the torn couch. In the semidarkness, the light from under the swaying lamp shade picked out a white rectangle on the table. I screwed up my eyes and squinted at the white patch until it turned into an envelope. There was the familiar imprint: "Notification of Death."

I opened it mechanically, out of force of habit, only to find another envelope inside it. The second envelope was glued shut. As I turned it over in my hands, I gasped like I'd been punched in the solar plexus: The Moscow address written on the envelope in a writing I recognized was my wife's address. Still not fully grasping what it meant, I ripped the envelope open with trembling fingers and out fell a piece of paper. The letters were small and crowded on top of each other, and although I was pretty sure that I knew what it said, I fumbled for my reading glasses. I hadn't worn them for a long time and I had no idea where they might be. I bent over toward the light and brought the letter as close to my eyes as possible.

These days I wear glasses all the time. It was clearly not the beginning of the letter, but I wasn't concerned about where it began. *I don't mean sunglasses, but ordinary ones for short sightedness, and sometimes I'm terrified that will make it even harder for you to recognize me when you come. I'm terrified in general about the changes in me that take place here without me really noticing. I am developing a different kind of vision, an internal one, because all the time, every second, in every conversation and every situation, you are always here, in the corner of my eye, to my right or to my left—it doesn't matter. I can actually see your face, and feel its warmth. As though my face is divided into two and one changes into yours. It's the way you see the face of a person standing at your shoulder when you are looking in a different direction. But when you come, I shall hold your hand all the time, and you'll walk beside me on the right so that if I turn my head I shall see your real face, and nothing will make me let go of your hand. I dreamt today that by some miracle I was in Moscow and I opened the door with my key and you were there to meet me. But your face was confused and embarrassed, and I saw that our home had changed and you had a different life, a life in which I had no place. Out of kindness you led me through to the back room, and I wasn't ever allowed out of it because I had no passport and was a citizen of a hostile state. So I quietly settled into this back room, allowing myself no more than to look out of the window at the familiar trees and the chimneys on the horizon. I got ready to go to bed feeling like a guest taken in out of charity, a disabled old distant relative who is allowed to stay but not to say a word.*

The final words blurred in front of my eyes because I was crying silently. I went on crying, angry that I couldn't stop, crying about my own death because I'd went on living without knowing this was the next life from which I could never get back to the first one, and there was no way back to myself, to the person I used to be, while the person I was now had turned into nothing, a nonentity. The efficient representative of our agency had filled out the funeral card and attached the letters I left.

I glanced at the date: 19 January 1975. Suddenly I remembered everything from beginning to end. This was the envelope I had taken out with me that ill-fated day and never posted at the main post office, because I met the old woman. "Am I really dead?"

I heard the strange sighs and soft little cries mixed with whispers again that seemed to answer my question. I looked around, trying to detect the source of the sound and spotted a chink of light at the bottom of the wall. There was no other light in the room. It was a different kind of light, not dim electrical light, but the kind of light I'd forgotten the name of. It was coming in from under the door, from under the door jammed shut with the slipper, the one I was forbidden to enter. I remembered the face of my hostess and her playfully threatening finger. I laughed spitefully. In two swift strides I was at the door and wrenched it open. A shaft of daylight blinded me, and only gradually did my eyes pick out the large familiar window, the undemanding sky and the large trees with their rustling leaves, and the crisp shape of the television tower on the horizon. I knew, I understood, I had no doubt, but still I gasped as I moved away from the window.

By the wall was a bed with a blanket that reached up to the shoulders I knew so well, the curve of the shoulder blade that I knew by heart, the tousled chestnut hair waiting for a familiar hand to stroke it. My wife lay there with her face turned into the crumpled pillow, sobbing and crying with a wet handkerchief clutched in her hand.

Quietly, so as not to frighten her, I tiptoed over to the bed, still smiling. There was a chair beside the bed, and on the chair a sealed envelope. I picked up the letter and laughed as I read my name on it in her writing. She had written me a letter after all. There were two stamps on the envelope: one showing Lenin in front of a power station, the other cosmonauts and a Sputnik in orbit. I cautiously sat down on the edge of the bed and put the letter in my pocket. Letters weren't needed any longer, and words weren't needed, at least not on paper. Words are written by fingers that have no one to caress. I reached out and stroked the tangle of hair.

"I'm here," I said. "I know," she said. "Have you forgiven me?" I asked. "Have you forgiven me?" she asked. "Yes," I said. "Yes," she said. "I'm not going away anymore, I've come back to you at last, there's nowhere else to go," I said. "There's nowhere else to go," she said. "I would have come to you." She was waiting to echo my words. "The only place to go to is the place where you still are," I said. "You still are here. To stay with the one you are willing to go away with," she said. "I didn't get out of bed, I thought you were walking about in the kitchen, making coffee, and then you would call me, and I would wake up completely," she said.

I folded back the blanket, and saw how the sun shone through her shirt. I bent over and brushed the back of her neck with my lips and felt the familiar warmth of her body. "I'll go into the kitchen now and make something nice for you, but don't you get up. I'll put the pillow behind you and we'll spread a napkin on your knees, and I'll sit beside you and tell you I couldn't sleep because I left without mending the lock on the door, and you have to put a slipper under it to stop it banging in the wind."

I bent down and pressed myself against her from behind, reached under the blanket and pulled up her nightshirt, and my hand moved up over the familiar curves until my palm was full. She stirred under my hand and moved closer to me. The door creaked behind me. "Close the door, what if someone comes in?" she whispered, turning round to reach me with her lips. "Who could come in, we're at home, aren't we?" I said, glancing round, and I tried to take her face in my hands. I saw her eyes smile trustingly for a second, and for an instant time came back together again. When I pulled her face toward me, she blinked, and once again I saw her eyes were red and tear-stained, but I smiled, because I knew that they would never cry again.

Suddenly her expression was distorted, at first in astonishment and revulsion, and then in terror. Her fingers tensed, her body jerked back toward the wall, and she pushed me so hard that I tumbled helplessly to the floor, clutching at the sheet as I fell.

I fell on my back and as the back of my head came down with a dull thud everything went hazy and her screams and screeches rang in my ears, above the sound of the leaves rustling and the wind whistling, a howl of terror and revulsion, the howl of a woman in shock: "Don't touch me! Oh God, don't touch me! Don't touch me!" The familiar world disappeared.

My own shivering woke me. The cold gripped my entire body. My head was splitting. I touched the back of my head. My hair was matted together. When I raised my hand to my eyes, the fingers were covered in blood. My other hand was clutching some kind of rag, and I began wiping my fingers on it; then I saw it was a handkerchief, my wife's handkerchief that I had taken from her clenched fingers. Now it was smeared with blood. As if the tears had not been enough. In the gathering twilight I tried to make out where I was. I was lying in an abandoned, half-empty house. Not even a house, but half-ruined walls with the skeleton of a roof and one wall completely missing. Through the gaping windowsills I could hear the voices of people walking along the street. I had no idea how I'd gotten there. I looked around, still clutching my head, and suddenly I shuddered in shame. My fly was open and my swollen shaft was sticking out. I leaped to my feet and zipped my trousers hurriedly. I figured that I'd wandered in half-delirious to relieve myself in a ruined house, stumbled over something, fallen, and banged my head. A gust of wind ruffled my hair, and I heard a rustling behind me. I spun around in panic, but it was only some scraps of old newspaper.

I pulled myself together and picked my way out of the ruin. Something glinted off from the corner, and when I looked closer, I saw a shard of a mirror that had miraculously survived on the wall. I peered into the mirror in the darkening air and started back from the reflection: An old man's ugly face stared back at me. I looked around, but there was no one behind me. I approached the shard again, and again the ugly old man moved forward to meet me. I tore the shard off the wall and looked at my reflection again.

"Why? What for?" asked the trembling old lips. I was clearly talking to myself by this time. I threw the shard aside and began walking round the ruined house, turning over everything and prodding the rotten old junk. In the doorway to the ruin, my foot stumbled over an old slipper, eaten away by time. The whole nightmare from beginning to end appeared before me in a single flash. I felt my wife's hands on my chest; her hysterical screeching rang in my ears. I gulped some air and dashed into the street.

I ran along the pavement, looking into the faces of the passersby hoping to see in their eyes whether they could see what had happened to me. But they regarded me with the indifferent curiosity normally shown to any man in an absurd hurry. How could they notice the change if they didn't know what I was like when I got there and what I would be like when I left? Maybe they thought I'd just arrived the way I looked now, or perhaps I'd grown like this by living here all my life, or rather, by dying here.

I dived into the public toilet and checked my face thoroughly in front of the mirror: these sagging lips of mine, this nose that droops down to my chin, these bags under my eyes, stretching halfway across my cheeks, these watery eyes. Look now for yourself what I saw there in the mirror. Don't be afraid, look! It's not your reflection, not yet. This is what happens to your face under the mask that they have fastened on you.

But let us get on with the ending. I hurried my steps to the familiar house of a friend. The door was opened not by my friend but his wife who officiously snipped, "We don't give to beggars." Should I have argued with her? The person who had to prove his lost identity no longer existed for them. And never would exist again. I couldn't prove that once there was a man who really wanted to prove what could only be proved by ceasing to be that man. I couldn't even prove that anything had to be proved. The witness had become the victim, and in so doing he'd destroyed the only evidence for the prosecution. And so the trial of emigration would adjourn for lack of evidence.

"Just a moment," I said to her, "I came to ask if you have the address of a friend of mine from Moscow. He mentioned your name in his letters, but then he moved. I'd like to visit him, just to see how he's settled into his new life." I hesitated before adding cautiously: "In fact, I have a letter for him, to be delivered by hand."

She looked at me suspiciously. "I'm afraid I can't help you. The police have already been here. You have to contact them. We phoned all the morgues. He'd certainly been acting strange, and that's putting it mildly. I told my husband for ages to get him a psychiatrist, but of course he didn't. He was seen yesterday."

"Near the post office?" I asked.

"Yes. How did you know? Anyway, since then no one has been able to find him anywhere." She was about to shut the door.

"I'm sorry, what day is it today?"

"Tuesday the twentieth," she said, wrinkling up her forehead. "Why?"

"What month?"

"January, of course!"

"Nineteen seventy-five?"

She looked at me dumbly. "What's wrong with you? Of course seventy-five!"

"All in one night," I mumbled.

"I beg your pardon?" she said.

"It's all right, I was talking to myself. Old men talk to themselves, you know."

I just stood there smiling stupidly at her, my hands unwittingly playing with the envelope I'd shoved in my pocket. Two bright stamps, with the cosmonauts and Lenin above my name and address. She glanced at the envelope.

"But you *have* your friend's address already!" she said in annoyance, and slammed the door in my face.

The bed, and my wife with her face in the pillow, and the chair beside the bed, and the envelope on the chair, the one I was just putting in my pocket, swam before my eyes. I tore open the envelope and pulled out a sheet of official letterhead. "You are hereby notified. . . ." I read, and on and on, to the words "sudden death" and "cardiac arrest" and "please inform us of the husband's whereabouts."

I went down the stairs, tearing the official notification of my wife's death into smaller and smaller pieces that drifted across the stoop until the draft caught them and they swirled up into the air like the snow that winter morning when I went down the Moscow stairs, leaving the door open, abandoning her in the empty room. I didn't need any written confirmation. I didn't need a crib sheet for my life. I needed a witness. I needed a witness who'd confirm the existence of that me who once believed my wife was alive despite all facts and figures. Now I am sitting here, and you don't believe me. The only person who'll believe me is that hateful woman. She's the only witness. So I have to wait till she gets here. She'll come all right, she'll come, she has nowhere else to go either. . . .

3. OFFER OF EMPLOYMENT

The stranger leaned back. Mark sat there half-drunk, staring past the old man at the door. It was noisy in the diner, and the air was thick with smoke. The day had gone by and Mark hadn't sent the letter to his wife; instead, he'd listened to yet another drunken confession from yet another madman, more nonsensical ravings, more gibberish.

Mark had to sober up quickly. The door opened and in she came. Mark recognized her immediately. There was the coquettishly cocked beret and the sharp knees and the suitcase. One glimpse of the suitcase was enough to set his shoulder aching. He sat up and waited to see what would happen next. Silence descended. Everyone seemed to be half-standing. She looked around with a smile, as everyone greeted her, frozen where they sat. They all seemed to know her as an old and honored guest. She made her way over toward Mark's table. Now she would beckon, and ask him to help her carry the suitcase. First you listen to someone else's words, then you begin to repeat them, then you begin to believe them, and then you begin to act on them to the very letter.

But no, she put down the suitcase without paying any attention to Mark and leaned over the old man. Mark breathed in the scent of her perfume. She looked at him and shook her head reproachfully, then sat down beside him. "Why did you get him drunk?" she asked in a rasping, weary voice. "No doubt he had enough time to tell you all kinds of nasty stories about me?

We've been searching for him since yesterday, phoned all the morgues. And it's not the first time. He's dead drunk again." She shook him by the shoulder and his head lolled to his chest. He could have been dead for all Mark knew. "He won't last long at this rate. Did he tell you about his wife too?" Mark didn't answer, but just stared, spellbound, into her face. "It's a tragedy what happens to these repatriates. I do volunteer work with the elderly and infirm. It's only to be expected. A man pulls up his roots and makes the leap, but left without his usual supports, he stumbles and falls, a long fall from the height of his newly acquired freedom, if you see what I mean. He's the one who gives us the most trouble. He has no desire whatever to make any kind of effort with himself and shake off this émigré depression. One can understand him, of course. His wife stayed behind in Russia, a sick old woman. Naturally he has psychological problems. But the only salvation from a disrupted personal life is in socially useful work. Our committee employed him to deliver letters. He can't work as a real mailman; his deliveries are almost a joke: to the chosen addresses, to elderly repatriates like himself. Perhaps we made a mistake. He listens to sick people's complaints, and they share each other's morbid fears." She broke off and looked at Mark as though she was assessing him professionally. "Why do you look so unwell? A young man of your age should be able to deal with the problems of assimilation. I think you're not eating regularly. And you probably stay out till all hours. At your age you need a regular daily routine. If you're interested, I can offer you some temporary work. And I have room for you to stay. You have higher education, don't you? You'd be copying out a few things, editing, modest work, but very worthy. Will you take it?"

MIND THE DOORS

These two guys were following me. I was certain of that. I tried to keep sight of them as I made my way through the busy Moscow street toward the Metro station, frightened and yet somehow fascinated. Their thuggishness was exotic, a cross between Afghan war veteran and British soccer fan. They braved the cold early spring drizzle without umbrellas, but looked as if a good raincoat—like the one on my back—might be appreciated. I had bought it the year before at an expensive place in Dublin. It made me 100 percent waterproof—that is, if it remained on my shoulders. It felt like I was being undressed by their furtive glances. The lecher and the street mugger, honed on a target, display almost identical bodily manifestations.

Perhaps I was just as paranoid as any other foreigner in Moscow, a city now swarming with criminals of every stripe. In any case, I was alarmed when the two youths followed me for not one but two blocks and then accompanied me down into the Metro station. It might have been a coincidence; Peace Prospekt was in fact the only station in the area. But then they might have taken a bus or a tram. But no, they opted for my means of transportation. I tried to laugh off my suspicions by reminding myself that I often suffer from that infantile aberration of narcissistic minds, where I imagine that whatever I do, wherever I go, others are watching and trying to do the same.

The idea of sharing the same route with these two boys was a bit awkward and funny. At this particular instant, my mind was full of lustful anticipation. I was on the way to meet my new lover. So it was a relief when I managed to lose "my tail," as they say in detective stories, while changing trains at Taganskaya station for the Marxistskaya line.

It might be fun, in passing, to attempt an unveiling of the mysterious logic underlying the decision to change certain place-names while leaving others untouched. Why, for example, was the ominous Dzerzhinsky Square changed to the sinister Lubyanka, while Taganskaya (the name of another former prison) and the perfidious Marxistskaya left for all eternity? It was nice they had not changed the name of the station where I was to meet my date. The Highway of Enthusiasts. Our mutual enthusiasm in bed was indeed unrivaled by my previous liaisons, so it was apt.

Thus those hoodlums were not the only reason I was anxious to get on the train still waiting at the platform at Taganskaya station. Most of us are familiar with that window of time when a train is about to depart and the doors are closing. You can already hear that sinister hissing of the pneumatic brakes. It is a time for action. I caught sight of the two who had been following me in precisely this situation. They stood inside the car beside the door. When they saw me on the platform, paralyzed with indecision, they each got hold of the sliding doors to keep them from closing.

"Hey, you, jump!" they shouted cheerfully, "Jump!" They waved their hands encouragingly.

"Don't do it, don't jump," the voice of wisdom was instructing me from the depths of my soul. "You should trust people," the opposing voice of humanity urged from another corner of my mind as I stared hypnotically at the ruddy faces of the two Russians waving their hands at me: "Jump, stupid, jump!" My whole life suddenly passed in a flicker before my eyes—a series of reckless jumps: emigration from Russia to Israel, a spell in France, a drastic move from France to England, changing addresses with the same ease as I change lovers. As I see now, my decision to visit my old country after so many years of separation was not the wisest step either. Neither of us, my country nor I, could recognize the other. I stood there in front of the alluring gap between the doors that invited me to jump into the hands of two people who, most probably, were hoping for just this opportunity to entrap me.

I hate to disappoint people. So I jumped.

I landed safely inside. The doors shut behind me with the bang of a prison gate. It was a close shave. I looked around with a triumphant smile of relief, huffing and puffing excitedly but proud of myself, looking somewhat stupid. The two I had suspected of malfeasance gave me friendly pats on the shoulder and returned to their seats. I was about to follow their example, choosing an empty seat in the half-occupied car. I took a step forward and immediately heard a frantic crackling sound behind me. I froze. I ventured a tentative step forward. I couldn't budge an inch, held back by some invisible hand. My body was inside the train all right, but not the tails of my raincoat.

I made yet another feeble attempt to free myself, and failed again, producing an even more bizarre sound. Presently, my predicament became evident to everyone in the Metro car. My few fellow travelers started to giggle, at first furtively, covering their faces with their hands. One sociopath roared with laughter. I shrugged my shoulders apologetically and tried on the brave ironical smile of a pupil showing off in class after being caught red-handed by the teacher. Never mind, I thought, maintaining a cheery expression. I knew that at the next stop I would be free.

When the train was about to pull up to the next stop, I readied myself to step aside when released, and to give way to the passengers entering the car. We stopped and a sonorous voice announced solemnly: "Illyich Square." The doors opened invitingly on the opposite side of the train. I gasped in disbelief but suppressed my dismay as I watched the faces of my fellow passengers staring at me, a fit of laughter just about to break, their faces reddening. The laughter spread as a few others joined the train at the Illyich Square station. ("Ilyich" in the station name refers, of course, to the great Vladimir Ilyich Lenin.)

"Mind the doors. Next stop Aviamotornaya."

I had traveled far from my now familiar London. I remembered all of a sudden that I had not fixed the front door lock, which had recently caused me to get locked in. Now I was locked in a Moscow train. I tried to pull the tails of my coat away from the doors once again. The attempt consisted of a little leap into the air, ballet style, my hands stretched wide as if embracing the brave new Russia. A horrible retch of tearing raincoat fabric made my heart sink. The sound was so obscene that I smiled apologetically. This sent the whole car into convulsions of laughter. Tears of joy appeared on many faces. I had made their day.

"It seems you have a choice here," said one of two louts who had lured me into this trap. "It's either the raincoat or freedom." It sounded like: "Your money or your life. Your coat or your love." He glanced at me with a hint of *schadenfreude* in his eyes. If I stood by my coat and failed to break free soon, I would risk missing my date altogether. We had agreed to meet at the exit of the station because she was afraid I might get lost among the chaotic conglomeration of faceless apartment blocks in her Moscow suburb. I imagined her standing there in the cold, scanning the crowds in vain. How could I let her know where I was? Where was I? There were only two more stops to go before I would have to get off this train, either with my raincoat or without it. The tunnel lights flickered incomprehensible messages to me through the train windows.

At Aviamotornaya station the wrong set of doors were used once again. The gates to freedom opened and closed again. A few more passengers joined the train and sat opposite me, as if they were at the theater; I was the new comic sensation. Each of them, having gradually discovered what had happened, would renew this rigmarole of exchanging glances first, and then turn their smug faces away with a suppressed giggle.

I looked pathetic.

One of the two comrades whom I held personally responsible for my disaster reassured me. "Don't you worry. There are only a few stations left before the last stop. The train goes to a yard outside of the city after that. If you scream your head off, somebody will come and let you out, for sure."

He was talking like a doctor to a sick child. This time I could muster only a faint smile. These two men might as well have been KGB agents, stalking foreigners, old style. Lefortovo, mind you, was the name of the whole area of Moscow we were passing through. During the Soviet rule, the place was notorious for the Lefortovo prison, a way stop for political dissidents on their way to labor camps. I had avoided that fate twenty years ago by emigrating. Now I am back where I supposedly belong, on the line to the Highway of Enthusiasts via Marxistskaya. They change names but the essence of Russian society remains the same: authoritarian, oppressive, mean. I was trapped on the line connecting Lubyanka's torture chambers with Lefortovo's prison cells. Old institutions, like old habits, die hard. My body was trapped by the cold iron body of the former Soviet-totalitarian make.

The sense of helplessness was overwhelming. Silence fell over my audience, as if the passengers had tired of my comic act. Now their eyes studied me with boredom and contempt. I was no longer a novelty; they knew that I was going to be with them all the way. I imagined how at the final stop the empty train would be taken to a remote corner of the tunnel and left there for hours in the darkness until some workers came along, checking cogs and nuts. They would discover me, strip me, take all my money and clothes, and then, if I was lucky, they wouldn't kill me but rather dump me somewhere on the railroad tracks, for me to find my way back to the light, back to life. My love at the Highway of Enthusiasts station would be long gone. She would feel betrayed.

That nightmarish scenario prompted my mind to rebel. I needed to break free, and my body jerked unconsciously, tearing a bit of my raincoat apart. It was hot. The back of my head was soaking wet with perspiration, and a trickle of sweat found its way down my spine as though it were raining inside the coat.

Suddenly I was struck by a brilliant idea. In a flash of inspiration, I took off my raincoat, leaving it to hang out from the clenched doors. In an instant I was standing next to the doors holding on to my precious possession by the sleeves. I still could not free it, but at least I was free to move about the train. I was amazed by my ingenuity and wondered why I had not thought of it before.

It was an illusory freedom. I couldn't abandon an expensive raincoat just like that, hanging forlornly, and I couldn't bare the mental rape by these former compatriots, who would all be doubtless envious of my Armani suit, the pink shirt with French cuffs from Jermyn Street, and my Church's shoes. I felt like an exotic creature at the zoo.

"Is he a foreigner or what?" asked a man opposite me, turning to the woman next to him who was evidently his wife. Old Soviet stock. Still, managing quite all right in the new economic order, to judge from their brand-new parrot-colored synthetic clothing.

"Of course he's a foreigner, stupid," replied the wife. "Don't you see the way he's dressed? Look at his raincoat."

"Why, nowadays our new Russians are as well dressed as any other foreigner. They can afford even more expensive things. Our lot have learnt how to make a buck or two," said the husband.

"Yes, at our expense," grumbled his wife. "Why haven't you figured it out yourself?"

"What?"

"How to make a buck or two."

"We aren't badly dressed either, are we? Don't you like my jacket? And yours? Bright and cheerful, not gloomy like this citizen. Everything's black as if there'd been a death in the family." They were discussing me as if I were dead.

"You don't understand," intervened a youngish man from an opposite seat. He brandished a French Resistance cap and a leather jacket. "You should always judge a man by his shoes. That's what my grandma taught me. This man's got foreign shoes," and he squinted his eyes at my Church's. He had brand-new Puma sneakers—a man of fashion in this part of the world.

"What about them?" asked the husband. "Black shoes. We had those in military school. Nothing fancy, just plain shoes." He was clearly puzzled.

"Don't you understand, stupid, what the young man's trying to tell you?" the wife said. "It's quality, not appearance, that counts. Beware the wolf in sheep's clothing." The Russian proverb, wrongly applied to this occasion, reminded me again of my own relative nakedness.

Yet another station with all ten syllables of its Russian

name was swallowed by the tunnel with no glimmer of hope for me.

"If he's a foreigner, how come he speaks Russian?" the husband did not relent. I had not uttered a single word up to this point, so it remained a complete mystery how they knew that I was a Russian speaker. Russian intuition, I suppose.

"So what? Lot's of foreigners study Russian these days," his wife retorted.

"What for?"

"What for? What for?! Because Russian is the most beautiful language in the world," cut in a man with a fedora hat with a thick batch of newspapers under his arm. "Don't you remember what the great Turgenev said about our grand and mighty mother tongue? What were you doing in school, masturbating?"

"Mind your language, citizen," put in another passenger in a beret. "Some of these foreigners don't give a damn about their mother tongue, or about their own mothers either. They only think about money and primitive self-gratification. That's all. They learn Russian because they think they can come and make an easy buck over here."

"Some of those foreigners don't care about money either. They come over here because they are bored to death in their own countries," said the young man in Pumas. "Life is too well regulated. Russia is chaotic and much harder, but more interesting too. They come here for fun."

"Our mafia men could give these disgusting foreigners their self-gratification, quick and painless," said the fedora hat. "Only the grave can straighten out a hunchback."

Everyone fell silent, contemplating this quick and painless

way of self-gratification and straightening my crooked back. I knew it was only another Russian proverb, but I touched my back furtively, checking the curve of my spine to be sure it wasn't a personal assault. The faces around me became gloomier, more sinister. It might have been pure imagination on my part, but it didn't make me feel any better. The wheels of the train were clicking to a hypnotic rhythm in the darkness of the tunnel. Above our heads the turbulent life of the big city was raging. We were running through the dark convolutions of the Russian unconsciousness.

"Anyway," the husband concluded his logical deliberations after a pause, "the only thing I know for sure is that it's impossible to say who is a foreigner and who isn't these days. And that's the trouble with this country."

"Foreigner? He's not a fucking foreigner, can't you see?" came in a hysterical shout from a man at the other end of the aisle, who was studying me with an attention bordering on disgust. He looked like a tramp in a raincoat made of something closely resembling tarpaulin, with an old cloth cap on his head. His emaciated face was twitching, as if insects were biting him. "I hate them. I hate them all. They make me sick. Sick. Sick." His face twitched again. He repeated every second word like an old gramophone record.

"Hey, take it easy, man," one of my two guardian angels barked in my defense. I was somewhat surprised, even grateful, but in my heart I knew that this pathetic madman was right. What kind of foreigner am I? Neither a foreigner, nor a Russian. A nonentity. A hybrid. A monster. My defender meanwhile told the twitching face to shut up.

"Why should I shut up?" he shrilled. "They were born here, they were looked after, Russia paid for their education and what-not, and then they betrayed us, they abandoned our motherland in her hour of need. Dirty capitalist money is not enough for them; they come back here greedy to corrupt our innocent souls with their rotten way of life. Why should we tolerate a provocation like that?"

Indeed, my visit to the Old Country was nothing but a provocation. We come back to the places of our youth to satisfy our curious vanity and vain curiosity. We want to be sure that we have grown out of our spiritual adolescence, and become wiser, richer, more important than those who stayed behind. We provoke them into telling us how different we have become, thus making us aware of our life achievements in faraway places while they have remained the same provincial failures. We come to pick for our own amusement the fruits of their starry-eyed adoration of our meteoric rise. And we abuse them.

"I spit on them. They make me sick, and I spit on these dirty traitors. Stinking Yids," he finally blurted out, and spat. It was a long-distance shot. But well aimed. It landed on the lapel of my raincoat.

"What d'you think you're doing, citizen?" The woman who a minute ago had reprimanded her husband for ignorance in sartorial matters now raised her voice. "It's an expensive item of clothing. You ruined it with your stinking spit."

"Not as stinking as these Yids stink," retorted the twitching citizen, fretting indignantly. That was only to be expected. There was a gasp from some of the passengers, amazed at this uncensored open manifestation of a familiar hatred. Other faces frowned in disapproval. It would be wrong and foolish to call "stinking Yid" an anti-Semitic remark. The "Yid" in the insult could be anyone—a Scot, a Frenchman, or indeed, a

Jew—anyone who had not shared in this wretch's miserable lot. There might just as well be a Martian standing in my place. The insult was in essence a desperate plea for compassion.

"With your lot around, soon nobody'll want to stay in this country. Or on this planet," added the young man with Puma sneakers. "If your lot comes to power I would be the first to leave Russia."

One individual voice of dissent would not change the character of the nation, of course. Still, I must say I was taken by surprise by this brave protest on my behalf coming from such an unexpected direction. But my very presence abused the trust of those few decent people who were prepared to defend me in front of the mob, those few who embraced me as a messenger of the bright future emerging from the West. There was no denying that I had come to Russia just for fun, for a kick, to satisfy my sexual appetite regardless of the consequences.

I wondered what my London neighbor, a psychoanalyst, would have made out of my ridiculous predicament, where the notion of journey, the promise of sexual intercourse, and the fear of castration merged neatly, and particularly given the fact that I was on my way to indulge in a treacherous act of adultery with the new wife of an old Moscow friend. The date was hastily arranged while he, a computer programmer, was away on assignment. This train of thought made me jerk again at the realization that I had neither her telephone number nor her address on me. How many hours would pass before I could contact her? Having failed to meet me at the Metro station, she would go back home thinking that I had decided to ditch her unceremoniously. She would be right. I felt my face turning red with unspeakable shame.

"It is political shortsightedness to put the blame for every-thing on Jews only," said the man in the fedora hat, with the voice of a lecturer in politics. "One should focus on more powerful and sinister enemies of mankind." And answering many an inquiring eye, the hat went on: "I mean, aliens. From other planets. Martians and others, things like that. Space in-vaders, you know," and he shrugged his shoulders, weary of explanation.

I knew I was not an extraterrestrial. But I was no less dan-gerous a creature: a time traveler. I belonged to a different tract of time—unfolding abroad—and I should not have come here, interfering with other people's lives, using the illegitimate knowledge of their past, present, and future. I had to keep my mouth shut and clear out, having left nothing behind that might alter the chain of events, the causes and the effect. I turned with renewed determination to those doors as tightly clenched as my teeth. I have to take with me all my belongings, "dead or alive," so to speak.

"Hey, comrade, shall we help you?" The familiar faces of my two minders, as I had started to call them, appeared at either side. Those I most distrusted were the first to help me out at this critical moment. I was moved enormously. My eyes filled with tears of gratitude. With trembling lips, I explained to them that I had had enough and had to get off at the next stop, tak-ing the coat with me at any cost. They positioned themselves at both sides of the doors trying to pull them apart while I tugged at the raincoat.

One day I would like to write an essay on how different national temperaments are reflected in the way the Metro doors shut in different countries. For example, in the London Underground the doors are lined with relatively soft rubber, so when a hand gets caught in between the doors, you can still pull it free without causing serious bodily harm. In Russia, the doors will cut your hand in half like a thief's caught hand in Saudi Arabia. I was amazed that my raincoat was still in one piece despite some minor damage.

"Hey, you," shouted one of my minders to the passengers standing in the aisles. "And you. And you too. What are you gaping at? Can't you see that the man is in trouble? Don't be bastards. Let's help our foreign comrade. He's got to get off at the next station. Come over here and give us a hand!"

At first one of the passengers, then another, answered this call and started to move toward our end of the car. More and more hands joined together, clutching the door opening in a collective attempt to break the iron grip. Soon I was in the middle of a crowd, huffing and puffing, advising and encouraging, pulling and pushing, jostling the doors. Human endeavor versus totalitarian machinery. I was surrounded by kind faces animated by collective effort on behalf of somebody they had never met before, someone who was not one of them, a foreigner, an alien. And still, they cared about him (me, that is). I was among friends. I recognized the familiar faces of the housewife and her husband, the face of the fedora and of Mr. Puma sneakers. Maybe my eyes were deluding me but I could swear I even saw the face of the man in the tarpaulin raincoat, his twitching features changed to an expression of remorse and repentance. I was no longer on an underground train; I was on a highway of enthusiasts leading to cloud nine.

And the miracle was taking place in front of our eyes: The raincoat began to emerge, inch by inch, from the iron jaws. It was like defusing a bomb. Time ticked away on the clock of the detonator. The train would be pulling into the station any moment now. We freed the raincoat a fraction of a second before the train stopped. A jubilant cry went up and I jumped to the left side of the car, waiting anxiously for the doors to open.

"This is the Highway of Enthusiasts. Please exit on the right side of the train," the recorded announcement informed us. I turned around. The doors on the other side, where I had stood imprisoned a moment ago, were gaping at me like the huge mouth of totalitarianism. The crowd gasped. The futility of human endeavor was written all over my face. I crossed the aisle and stepped out of the train the way a defeated wrestler might leave the ring. Standing on the platform, I watched through the windows of the departing train the dear faces of my fellow passengers, waving farewell in an impulsive manifestation of brotherhood. The effort had been futile, perhaps, but the sensation of taking part in it will stay with me forever.

The train disappeared into the tunnel, and with a melancholic sigh I put on my poor raincoat and looked around for the exit. I had not lost all of my fellow travelers. My faithful companions, witnesses of all my trials and tribulations, stood with me on the platform like angels emerging from a heavenly dream. I knew now how deceived I had been by their thuggish looks. I smiled warmly and shook their hands, thanking them from the bottom of my heart for the generosity of brotherly feelings they had demonstrated during our eventful journey. Thanks to them, I had experienced that forgotten sensation of being part of a larger family, of the real Russian hidden from the eyes of foreigners. They were smiling, too, shy smiles, like those of modest people who feel slightly embarrassed when unduly praised.

"About this thingy," said one of them, tentatively fingering the lapel of my raincoat.

"Yes, how about it?" said another.

"What about it, indeed?" I was confounded, my tone echoed his.

"Will you take it off yourself?" asked the first.

"Or should we help you?" suggested the other. They removed the precious raincoat from my shoulders with the elegance of cloakroom attendants. The crowd on the platform passed by, oblivious or indifferent to what was happening in front of them. I was standing there without my raincoat, exposed to the elements, but right on time, ready to meet my date. Or to avoid the situation and take the next train home.

On the other side of the platform the train was about to depart, hissing ominously. My two friends were just going to make it. The doors closed behind them with a prison like metallic bang, leaving the tail of my raincoat protruding obscenely.